DEATH IN THE CREASE

· · · · · · · · · · · · · · · · ·

The Pro Book Two

RICHARD CURTIS

WOLFPACK
PUBLISHING
— EST 2013 —

WOLFPACK PUBLISHING
— EST 2013 —

Death In The Crease

Paperback Edition
Copyright © 2020 (As Revised) Richard Curtis

Wolfpack Publishing
6032 Wheat Penny Avenue
Las Vegas, NV 89122

wolfpackpublishing.com

Paperback ISBN 978-1-64734-145-9
eBook ISBN 978-1-64734-058-2
Library of Congress Control Number 2020944885

DEATH IN THE CREASE

. . . .

This one's for David and Anita Saunders

CHAPTER I

· · · ·

There's a famous poem that starts, "April is the cruelest month." That may be true for poets but in my line of business—professional sports—April is the most happy month. It's the month in which baseball season opens, basketball and hockey playoffs get underway, golf tournaments make a swing into the thawing north, tennis and track come outside, and sports groupies strip down to the minimum apparel tolerated by law. In April, we shed the morbidity of winter and join hands in a kind of orgiastic communion of spectatorship. It is no accident that all of this coincides with the Easter and Passover holidays, themselves vestiges of profligate fertility rites conducted during planting time in days of yore. Myself, I look forward to my vacation for April. Let others winter in Palm Beach or summer in Ireland; I take two or three weeks in mid-April through early May and I attend the games. If I can't cadge free tickets from my friends in league or commission offices, I buy them at the box office, if I can't get them there, I buy them from scalpers at outrageous tariffs, if the scalpers don't have them, I watch the games on television, sometimes firing up three sets at once so I can catch every moment of action from every source.

Obviously, the guy who wrote "April is the cruelest month" never sat in Shea Stadium when Pearl Bailey threw out the first ball or stood for Kate Smith's rendition of "God Bless America" at the opening round of Stanley Cup Playoffs. And just as obviously, anybody who waxes as rhapsodic as I do about April is going to be pretty ticked off if something comes up to prevent him from indulging his passion for sports that month. It shouldn't be difficult to imagine, then, how profoundly upset I was to get a phone call from Vincent Sturdevant, president of the National Hockey League, asking if I'd be willing to undertake a secret assignment that happened to coincide with these two or three weeks a year for which I live. But Sturdevant's request was couched in terms equivalent to a command and a man in my position could not afford to refuse a command from a man in his, at least, not out of hand. I was obliged to fly up to Montreal where the NHL is headquartered and hear the proposition out. He would not give me a clue about it over the phone.

Which is how I came to be sitting in the death-seat of a windy, creaky, and none-too-stable MG darting in and out of the interstices between leviathan gasoline trucks and tractor trailers coming off the Triborough Bridge heading for Long Island, a little before eight on a Friday morning in mid-April. The driver was my secretary Trish and possibly the only thing that kept my rage and depression from being total was the sight of her long legs, exposed to within a millimicron of her crotch, operating the pedals of the car.

At any other time, this sight is one of life's keener pleasures. And if the girl is a horrendous driver, which Trish was, this diversion also saves wear and tear on the nerves. You don't have to watch the road, ducking and flinching with each narrowly-averted catastrophe; you just fixate on those dimpled knees at the juncture of well-muscled calves and alluringly tapered thighs as her feet depress clutch, throttle, and brake in ever-changing combinations, like a dancer improvising to music she's never heard before. And if she rams into an ice-cream truck or a Greyhound bus, you go to your death oblivious, your last conscious thought being how great those legs would be wrapped around your waist as you plumb the velvet delights between them.

I was never to plumb Trish's velvet delights. Oh, they were there for the plumbing any time I wished, as she was always making abundantly clear to me with bold displays of her body and verbal invitations of astonishing directness. But I had learned shortly after going into business for myself that while a good bedmate is as ephemeral as a mayfly, a good secretary is forever. The quickest way to lose a gal friday is to take her home with you for the night. Thus when Trish came along, displaying a splendid repertoire of secretarial skills, I decided to forgo the pleasure of seduction in deference to the higher pleasure of a well-run office and a correct lunch order every day. It was just my bad luck that Trish was the kind of girl whose reaction to a man's denial is to redouble her efforts to get him into bed. As a result, I had spent the two years since hiring her in a state of semi-satyriasis.

As she steered the MG into the fast-moving outbound traffic on the Van Wyck Expressway, I removed my eyes from her legs and shifted them to her face, a gamin-like oval with a corona of blond ringlets, intense gray-green eyes, and a soft mouth that concealed a tongue as filthy as a stevedore's when its owner was aroused. At the moment that tongue was flicking frenetically between compressed lips as Trish concentrated on negotiating her boyfriend's rattletrap as far as La Guardia Airport.

"May I ask you a question?" I said, trying to suppress my strong curiosity.

"Sure."

"How come you offered to drive me to the airport?"

"I thought it was the secretarial thing to do."

"You know perfectly well I prefer a taxi to you. You know perfectly well I'd prefer Evel Knievel to you."

She feigned hurt. "I thought my driving had improved."

"Is there something you want to talk to me about? And for Christ's sake, don't take your eyes off the road to answer the question! You know what I look like." The little car, having drifted into the middle lane while she was looking at me, now lurched like a water bug as she overcorrected, almost slamming us into the right-hand guard rail.

"Something I want to talk to you about? Why, no," she said airily. Too airily to be true. "Of course, I'm curious about this Montreal business."

"You know as much about it as I do. Vincent Sturdevant called me yesterday afternoon and asked if I could fly up to Montreal first thing this morning."

"And all he said was that it's official National Hockey League business?"

"That and that I'd be well paid for my time."

"But what do you think it is?"

I shrugged. "We don't represent many hockey players. At first I thought, maybe one of them is in some kind of trouble. But that wouldn't merit a drop-what-you're-doing call from the prime minister of hockey."

"Maybe one of our clients is in big trouble."

I shook my head. "I called all of them last night but nary a one could think of anything that might give the league serious cause for complaint. Stay on your right," I said as a sign saying "94th Street" came into view. "The airport turnoff is just a few hundred yards past this next exit."

We glided past 94th street and onto the exit road, then bore right in the direction of the Eastern Airlines wing of the terminal. Trish pumped the brake pedal heavily as we found ourselves at the end of a long file of cars and taxis inching around a U-shaped approach road. I tapped my overnight bag impatiently. It wasn't just fear of missing my plane but the realization I'd be trapped in the car with Trish for at least five minutes and I was certain from little nuances in her behavior that she was going to hit me with some major, urgent problem which had to be resolved this very moment. It wouldn't be the first time she'd pulled such a stunt and I braced myself against it. With all the other weighty things I had on my mind, I didn't need any excess emotional baggage this morning.

Sure enough, she turned to me and fluttered her eyelids. "Actually, there was something I wanted to talk to you about."

I sighed. "What is it, a raise? I raised you five dollars six months ago. The accountant says—"

"No, it's about Dennis."

"Dennis? What about Dennis?" Dennis Whittie was the new assistant I'd hired. A former backcourt man for the Virginia Squires, he'd faded into obscurity after dislocating a hip in a game against the New York Nets. I'd lost track of him and figured he'd turn up one day tending bar in Harlem or running a MacDonald's franchise somewhere, as is the fate of so many good but not super professional athletes when their playing days are over. Then he'd turned up in a most unexpected place, as a member of a kind of secret service unit connected with the office of the Commissioner of the American Basketball Association. Apparently, several sports commissions have similar task forces retained to hunt and destroy "irregularities," like drug use or gambling among players before they become public scandal. Dennis had helped me locate a kidnapped client and I liked his intelligence, doggedness, and the cool disdain with which he kicked adversaries in the nuts.

And so when it came to pass that my agency, Red Dog Players Management, began to prosper to the point where I needed help negotiating contracts and managing athletes, I asked Dennis if he'd like to come into the firm as my assistant. He was to start work Monday.

"What is he going to do?" Trish asked.

"He's going to help out. You do admit we need help, don't you?"

"Oh, sure."

"I should think you'd be thrilled, since you're so loaded with work."

"Oh, I'm pleased all right."

"Thrilled is the word I believe I used. Why are you only 'pleased' and not 'thrilled'?"

We advanced a few car lengths. "I guess I don't understand why, if I'm so overburdened, you're the one who gets an assistant. Shouldn't I be the one who gets one?"

"What would you do if you had one?"

"Some of the more glamorous work," she said forthrightly.

"I can't afford the luxury of hiring an employee to do glamorous work. I made it clear to Dennis that until our agency is high on Fortune magazine's list of five hundred top service corporations in the country, he was going to have to do a lot of crap-work. He understands that and I want you to understand it, too. As far as I'm concerned, Dennis is just a glorified secretary." That was not strictly true but I said it to mollify Trish, whose passionate views on sexual equality in business were well known to me.

"That's exactly it," she said, pounding the steering

wheel. "Why can't I be a glorified secretary?"

"Because somebody's got to order coffee and danish in the morning."

I bit my lip as soon as I said it and I could see a flush of anger climbing up her throat. "Aha!" she said triumphantly.

"Aha yourself."

"Is Dennis going to order coffee and danish in the morning?"

"Well...no."

"Aha again, you sexist bastard."

I sighed again, only louder. "What do you want?"

"Some responsibilities."

"But you're only a woman," I said.

Had she been looking at me, she'd have seen the teasing smile on my face when I made the remark. But she was watching the cab in front of us. Like most fanatics, she had no sense of humor when it came to her cause. Her head snapped around and she looked daggers at me. Then she reached for the ignition key, turned the motor off, parted her thighs, inserted the key between them, and crossed her legs. "Take that back," she said.

"Jesus, Trish, I was just kidding. Come on, the line's moving."

"I want some responsibilities," she repeated. A twenty-yard gap had opened in front of us, and horns behind us were beginning to blare. I looked at my watch. My plane left in about four minutes.

"Trish, stop fucking around."

"I'm not fucking around, Dave. Look, I've been with you...what, a little over two years now? I know every function of our agency. I know sports and I know athletes. I've got a good head for business. I'm attractive and charming, if I do say so myself. In negotiations, I'm tough but diplomatic. And I'm dynamite in bed, though that's something you wouldn't know. Above all, I'm ambitious. If I thought I'd go to my grave having achieved nothing beyond remembering who takes 'light' and who takes 'regular' and who takes 'black,' I'd leave you so goddam fast I'd be halfway to L.A. before the door slammed."

"My plane leaves in two minutes," I said, estimating the gap between our car and the cab in front of us at fifty yards. The cacophony of horns behind us had reached a mad crescendo.

"What's it gonna be, boss?" she said coolly.

"You had to spring this on me now."

"I've tried to talk to you before but you always put me off."

"I miss this plane, it's your job," I said.

"Just say the magic words."

A TWA 727 screamed into the sky, emphasizing my growing desperation. I looked at my watch. The second hand swept around the dial toward a missed appointment. "All right, all right. I'll tell you what. You want feminism, go get me some women athletes. Any you get, you can handle."

She clapped her hands. "You mean that?"

"The key, Trish."

"Oh, you bubby!" She leaned over and kissed me.

"The key, Trish. And please don't call me bubby. I hate that word."

She uncrossed her legs and spread her thighs, looking at me in mute invitation. I reached across the gap between seats and inserted my hand between her thighs. She closed her eyes and sucked in her breath.

Suddenly a dark shadow fell across us. It was the driver of the car behind us, a huge lumber-jacketed guy with a moonface and freckles. He looked down at the admittedly compromising sight of my hand between Trish's legs. "You couldn't wait till you got to the parking lot?"

"She has my key," I explained sheepishly. My fingers touched metal and I withdrew the key and showed it to the guy. "See?"

"Just move out, will ya, fachrissakes?" He spun to walk away.

"Go get fucked, Mac." Trish snarled, starting the car.

He wheeled and gaped unbelievingly at Trish as if she were a dummy and I the ventriloquist. Then he lunged for the car. Trish gunned the throttle and jerked us with a screech into first gear. He ran ten yards after us, then stamped his feet and walked back to his car. We wheeled around the rest of the U and jounced up to the Eastern Airlines terminal.

"You're still a fantastic bubby!" she shouted at me as I dashed up the stairs.

I barely made the plane, a 727 that seemed to begin its descent into Montreal a scant few minutes after it reached cruising altitude. It was a splendid April day, clear as spring water except for that brown haze of polluted air trapped at about fifteen thousand feet that seems to have become a permanent smudge across the northeastern skyscape. Other than that, conditions, as they say, were CAVU—Ceiling And Visibility Unlimited—and I felt a glow of wellbeing that even the contretemps with Trish could not diminish.

In fact, Trish's little act of rebellion could, I decided, produce some highly desirable results. For some time, I'd been distressed by the gap in my client list created by the absence of female athletes. My young agency had been picking up momentum in the last year, due largely to my highly publicized acquisition of Richie Sadler, perhaps the finest basketball prospect in decades, as a client, and the sensational terms I'd secured for his services. The number of athletes I represented and managed had almost doubled in the last year and I now had a solid list of baseball, football, and basketball players, a good sampling of hockey and tennis players and golfers, plus a miscellaneous sprinkling of professional track and field men, boxers, racing-car drivers, and even soccer players.

What I had damn few of, though, was women athletes—golfers, tennis players, track-and-fielders, hell, even jockeys. This omission was not by design, it's simply that they didn't come my way. Yet salaries and prize purses for women had been growing at a remarkable rate. Between increased media exposure and women's militancy, women had become a significant force in sports and not just a charming novelty. It seemed a shame, I'd reflected lately, that I wasn't cashing in on some of that action. So, if Trish could bring it in—well, God bless her.

Hockey was another area where I held weak cards. Again, it wasn't that I turned hockey players away, it was just that not many came to me, to begin with. Also, I had to admit to a certain prejudice against the sport that reflected itself in the low priority I gave it in my hunt for new clients. To an American, and a Texan at that, hockey had a faintly alien flavor. Though of course there were American teams and since expansion of the National Hockey League in 1967 and the more recent establishment of the rival World Hockey League, that number had grown but I never could get my head into the mystique of the game. Hell, there was now a hockey team in Dallas-Fort Worth, my home turf, but at the one game I'd attended I felt stranger than a Hindu at a barbecue. Hockey belonged to the Canadians; for me it was an acquired taste and something I took interest in only because my line of work required it. It wasn't in my blood the way football and baseball are.

Still, I'd have liked to be deeper into hockey and it was thus with considerable interest that I stepped off the plane at Dorval. The airport was about thirteen miles out of the center of Montreal and I boarded a bus, having told Vince Sturdevant not to bother picking me up since I wasn't sure which flight I'd be on.

The trip into the city gave me some more time to speculate on this mysterious mission. I hadn't a clue as to what Sturdevant could want with me but I figured that a connection with the kingpin of professional hockey couldn't hurt by any means. Actually, kingpin was hardly the word for Vincent Sturdevant. From what I'd heard about him, he was a pale shadow of his predecessor, Clarence Campbell, who'd run the game with a mailed fist for decades.

Unfortunately, as so often happens in a time of instability in the sports world, a weak man had been chosen as a compromise among a multitude of warring factions. Campbell's crown fell not merely to Vincent Sturdevant's shoulders but to his ankles. Sturdevant quickly proved to be a trimmer, adjusting his sails to every shift of the wind and basing all his decisions, when he was capable of making any at all, on the decibel count of the interest groups pressing him. Whoever ranted loudest inevitably won the decision. When it got around that that was how you got your way with Vince Sturdevant, everybody started yelling at him. The result was near paralysis of leadership.

The NHL's central headquarters were ensconced on the nineteenth floor of the Sun Life Building, a soaring structure of modern design projecting its face over Dominion Square. The anteroom was spacious and plush, done in rosewood paneling and royal blue carpeting. On the walls were hung blown-up action photos in vivid color of some of hockey's all-time greats and all-time great moments—Red Kelly, Jean Beliveau, Bobby Orr, Gordie Howe, Terry Saw-chuck, Toe Blake, Bobby Hull, Glenn Hall, Stan Mikita. You didn't have to be a hockey nut for your heart to quicken at the sight of Terry Sawchuck suspended straight-out like a hyphen in front of his net, the puck perched precariously on the tip of his glove (lots of white showing, as they say in baseball) and those fierce eyes glowing beneath that army crewcut. Or the famous "Kraut" line of Boston, Bauer, Schmidt and Dumart swarming past the Montreal net with sticks upraised in triumph. I became so engrossed in the exhibit I didn't hear the receptionist summoning me.

She was a dark-haired French-Canadian girl with warm brown eyes and a modest smile. Montreal girls are every bit a match for their New York counterparts in beauty, and in comportment, I find them superior—more genuine and less sex-obsessed. I think it's because their religious tradition is stronger than ours and they remind me of some girls in the Bible Belt of Texas. They go about their business with brisk professionalism, which gives them a special allure. The girl who's all up-front is less interesting than one who makes you work to find out what she's like deep down. And deep down—well, Derek Sanderson once said that when he was playing in Toronto the girls were so terrible he and his teammates had to import some from Montreal. But I digress.

"Monsieur?" she said again.

"Um, Monsieur Sturdevant, s'il vous plaît. Je m'appelle Monsieur Bolt," I said, exhausting my French vocabulary and hoping the girl wasn't too chauvinistic about her native language, as many folks from Quebec are. French doesn't come naturally to me. Spanish is my second language, as it is for all Anglos; I learned it on the laps of our criadas and dueñas on the ranch and picked up some German during my military hitch. Also, I know some bastard Yiddish which I learned from Trish and which is a prerequisite for survival in New York City. But French just doesn't dance trippingly on my tongue, as the receptionist, smothering a laugh, recognized. "Monsieur Sturdevant will see you at once," she said, pronouncing it "Stoor-day-vaw."

She ushered me to a door behind her, which opened on a large bullpen where a dozen people performed clerical tasks with an efficiency muted by deep carpeting and rich flocked wallpaper. The contrast between the violent sport of hockey and the subdued atmosphere of the office that controlled it was remarkable.

"Past zose cubicles, turn right, and you'll find Monsieur Stoor-day-vaw's office at ze end of ze hall," she said with a wave of a pretty arm.

"Merci beaucoup," I said, dredging up one last phrase.

I proceeded down a corridor flanked by glass-enclosed cubicles, sticking my nose in one or two to sniff the activity within—immense copying machines here, a printing press hammering out bulletins there, a tomblike archive, a frenetic mailing room. Then I hung a right and entered a more dignified hallway where the executive offices were located. The walls were hung with pictures of some of the league's more famous arenas: Montreal's Forum, Maple Leaf Gardens, Boston Garden, Madison Square Garden, Chicago Stadium, and such spanking new sports complexes as Jack Kent Cook's spectacular Forum, home of the Los Angeles Kings, the Spectrum in Philadelphia, the Omni in Atlanta, and Nassau Coliseum, home of the Islanders, all monuments to the explosive expansion of basketball and hockey in the last decade.

The door of the President's office opened just as I was raising my knuckles over the gilt lettering and I was face to face with Vincent Sturdevant. He was a youngish man for so important an executive, in his early forties. He was tall and broad-chested and I remembered he'd played defense for the Detroit Red Wings for a couple of years before retiring for the pleasures of coaching and, finally, front office work. Yet his wide shoulders were rounded as if the burdens and responsibilities he'd taken on so recently were already aging him. He had an unsightly premature middle-age spread that made his suit look ill-fitting and cheap. His face was soft and round and his eyes bland and a little fearful. He blinked a lot in flutters and he sometimes flinched, I was to discover, when you made a sudden movement. It was as if he were afraid you were going to lunge for him. The impression I'd gotten from a hasty look at my files the night before was confirmed in a glance; this was a man completely cowed by the bullies who ran the league's constituent franchises. He took my hand and pumped it and flashed a bright public-relations smile, thoroughly insincere and joyless.

His office was bright and spacious and shimmered with strong noonday light filtering through gauzy golden curtains. The predominant color was red and the motif of the carpet and wallpaper was the red oak leaf, Canada's national symbol, overlaid on golden fleurs-de-lis. The walls were hung with highly stylized paintings of hockey players in action and on pedestal-like fixtures between them stood a collection of trophies. The room was divided into two separate areas, the working one consisting of a desk surrounded by four plush chairs and backed by a bookshelf-bar-trophy case and a sitting one with comfortable chairs and sofas and a huge marble table on which sat a replica of the Stanley Cup filled with bright spring flowers. Two people sat on the sofa sipping white wine. I recognized the man but the woman was unfamiliar to me.

The man was Buzzy Chambers, owner of the Denver Rockies, an expansion team two or three seasons young.

Buzzy was a robust guy in his late thirties who'd inherited a mining fortune and bought himself a hockey franchise with it. Though, like many of the new breed of owners, he was a dabbler who knew little about the fine points of the game, he'd had the good sense to hire a top coach, Henri Richard, the retired Canadian great. Richard had not only brought instant glamour with him but after one ignominious year (which is all but mandatory for expansion teams, since they're invariably composed of green rookies, pensioners hauled out of retirement, unhappy draftees from other clubs, and, I sometimes think, convicts, slaves, and impressed sailors), had made his boys contenders. Buzzy was a handsome, athletic young man with long hair and a golden beard and wire-rimmed glasses who could easily be mistaken for a rock musician. Though on the two occasions I'd met him (one of his goalies was a client of mine), he'd struck me as a pleasantly disposed guy, today he looked ill at ease, sitting on the edge of the sofa and pulling at his drink in birdlike sips.

Beside him, looking not quite as uptight but extremely serious, a raven-haired woman sat appraising me with dark eyes. I put her age at just around the fulcrum of thirty. Her figure was definitely and most agreeably, that of a young girl but there was a depth in her eyes and in the taut line of her mouth that bespoke experience and maturity. I guessed she was married, and my eyes flashed to her hands, which gracefully caressed her crystal wineglass. There was a gold band on the ring finger of her right hand, meaning—what? Divorced? Separated? Widowed? Whatever it was, I was immediately interested in her. She wore a yellow linen skirt and a sheer cotton blouse with those maddening pockets over the breasts for girls who like to go braless but don't like to be obscene about it. After a quick survey of her legs, which were long and prettily turned and modestly pressed together, my eyes returned to her jet-black hair. It was combed in a glossy pageboy that surrounded her oval face like a monk's cowl and was the most striking feature of this striking woman.

"I believe you know Buzzy Chambers," Sturdevant said, leading me to Buzzy for a pressing of flesh, "but I don't think you've ever met Ellen Boudreau."

"I've never had the good fortune," I said, taking her soft left hand in mine.

Sturdevant gave a long hollow laugh. "Ah, that's right, you're a Southern gentleman. Gallantry and all that."

Ellen Boudreau gave my hand a businesslike squeeze. "Mr. Bolt, how do you do."

"Is it Miss or Mrs. Boudreau?" I asked.

"Mizz," she said, unsmiling. Her voice had a husky, cloudy quality I've always adored since my childhood crush on June Allyson.

"Ellen is an editor with E. J. Streeter, the New York publisher," Sturdevant explained, crossing to his well-stocked bar. "Will you have some white wine with us?"

"I don't hold liquor very well before one o'clock," I said.

Sturdevant looked at his watch. "It's a quarter of."

"Then I'll take the risk."

I sat down on a chair facing Buzzy and Ms. Boudreau. While Sturdevant tinkered at the bar, Buzzy and I exchanged awkward pleasantries. Buzzy said, "So? How's things?"

"Things are dandy. How's it look for the Rockies? They're what, two games out of second place?"

"Three as of last night. The Blues ate us alive."

"How's Paul Beauregard working out?" Beauregard was my client, the team's new goalie.

"Learning fast."

"Too bad about Guy Laclede," I said matter-of-factly. Laclede, the Rockies' regular goalie, had been killed in an auto accident a few weeks ago. It was his place that Beauregard had taken.

There was an exchange of significant looks between Buzzy and Ellen, some shifting of legs and clearing of throats. I wondered if I'd said something improper.

"It's interesting you mention that," Sturdevant said, returning with a brimming glass of yellow wine, "because that's what this whole thing is all about."

The drum of my memory bank spun and the readout displayed what little I knew about Laclede. He'd been a goalie with the Chicago Black Hawks, then was traded a couple of years ago to the newly formed Rockies after the Black Hawks lost to the New York Rangers in one of the wildest playoffs in the history of the game. Laclede had lost three of the four games in the finals and, with the coach and another goalie, had been summarily, and, I'd thought, unjustly given the boot. This year he had been leading the Rockies to a playoff berth when his car ran off a cliff in the mountains around Boulder, Colorado. That was all I knew about him except that he was neither great nor terrible—just another competent goalie in a big world and destined for obscurity when his playing days were over. The biggest ripple caused by his death was the inconvenience it caused the Rockies until they found a replacement.

So, I couldn't imagine what it was about him that merited a summit conference. One possibility did flash into my mind, however, "Does somebody suspect foul play or something?" Another surge of squirming and exchanged looks told me I was on the right track.

Sturdevant shrank and looked around the room as if it were bugged. "One step at a time, Dave. Before we get into it, I want you to understand that this is a matter of the highest sensitivity. Without meaning to sound dramatic, it's so potentially dangerous that any leak to the outside world could damage the institution of hockey irreparably. We've got to keep it 'in the family', as it were."

I scratched my head. "Then why call on me? I'm not 'in the family'."

"Well," Sturdevant said, "I do have a staff who do investigatory work for me regularly but all of those guys are well known to the players and management and their presence might prove alarming. You're relative unknown in hockey circles, yet because you're a players' agent you have a natural reason to, uh, go around."

"But how'd you come to pick me?"

"Niles Lauritzen told me you'd handled an extremely delicate matter for the ABA last year—he didn't tell me what but he said you'd tackled it with great skill and discretion. Niles's praise stuck in my head and when this… um…matter came up, I remembered you."

The reference was to the kidnapping of my client Richie Sadler, which I'd brought to a happy conclusion at the cost of a few lacerations, contused testicles, a few other bruises, and a price considerably lower than the three-million-dollar ransom his captor was asking for him.

"That's very flattering, Mr. Sturdevant," I said, "but one solved crime does not a detective make."

"Of course not, but this is a matter that calls for a very different approach than the kind used by conventional investigative bodies. From what Niles told me about you, you fit the bill better than anyone I can think of. But in case you're still skeptical, I had another talk with Niles yesterday and he said the promise of a high fee would make you decidedly more amenable to suggestion than you might otherwise be."

I smiled and said, "Shall we get down to business?"

Sturdevant gestured at Ellen Boudreau. "I'll let Ellen fill you in."

Ellen put her wineglass down, reached into her purse and withdrew a pack of Winchesters. Three hands with cigarette lighters materialized under her nose. Buzzy Chambers got there first. She touched his hand lightly to steady the flame, then drew a deep draught of aromatic smoke into her lungs and began to talk. The husky sonority of her voice was enchanting and I noted a peculiar inflection of the ou sound, making "about" come out sounding like "aboot." I guessed she was Canadian. At that moment, I'd have preferred hearing Ellen Boudreau read the Montreal phone directory over Joan Sutherland singing the Queen of the Night.

"For about seven years I was a reporter for the Toronto Globe and Mail. I was also a hockey nut; they even let me do hockey reporting, which is rare for a woman. Guy Laclede was an old and dear friend of mine and we often talked about his writing a book about hockey." She tapped the ash of her Winchester into a little silver tray on the coffee table. "When I moved to New York City, I took a job with Streeter. They've always been very big on sports books and when I told them I knew a lot of hockey players, they asked me to develop some book projects. I thought immediately of Guy and we came up with an idea for a book about life on an expansion team. I talked to Guy and he was thrilled with the idea but he also said he wanted to expand the book into an overall exposé of hockey. We said, so much the better. So we put him under contract."

She drained her wine and three hands reached for the bottle in the ice bucket. This time I got there first.

"Thank you. Well, the season began and just after the Christmas holidays we became curious to know how Guy was coming along. So we asked him to send in what he'd done." She tapped a heavy manila file folder resting against her ankles. "He delivered three chapters, plus a rough outline of what was to be in the rest of the book."

"And?"

"And it was just what we'd been hoping for. Lots of inside stuff, juicy anecdotes, and spicy gossip—just marvelous. In fact, some of it was so frank, we'd have probably had to change a lot of names to keep from being sued."

It was now obvious what she was leading up to and why Laclede's death had triggered a panic in hockey's highest precincts. "You think that someone mentioned in the book killed Guy Laclede to prevent him from publishing…"

"You're anticipating, Mr. Bolt," Ellen said sternly. "And actually you're only half right. We believe that it's someone not mentioned in the book who may have killed Guy."

"You got me buffaloed there," I said. "Unless you mean that someone who knew that Guy was writing this book got scared that Guy would reveal a nasty secret and bumped him off first."

"That's approximately right," she said.

I turned to Sturdevant. "So you want me to find out who killed Guy Laclede."

"Yes," Sturdevant replied, "but that's not as important as finding out what was the reason for his murder."

"Ah, then it wasn't just some nasty little secret, like somebody sleeping with somebody else's wife or something."

"If it were," said Sturdevant, "I wouldn't have lost as much sleep as I've lost this past week." He looked at Ellen. "Would you mind reading that passage to Dave?"

She put the manila folder on the table, unwound the string, and pulled out a sheaf of manuscript about an inch thick. She placed all but the last few pages, face down on the coffee table, then scanned the remaining pages, explaining,

"What I'm looking at is Guy's outline of the unwritten balance of the book. In it, he says—ah, here it is."

I leaned forward with elbows on knees as Ellen read the passage for which Guy Laclede may have paid with his life.

"'In this chapter, I propose to expand some remarks about gambling I made in chapter three. Until very recently, the sport of hockey never attracted big-time gambling and the gangsterism that goes with it. There are several reasons why. For one thing, big-time sports gambling is almost strictly an American phenomenon, not a Canadian one. But Americans didn't bet much on hockey until lately because they didn't think of it as a native sport. Except for the cities of Boston, New York, Chicago, and Detroit where there were NHL franchises, most Americans weren't exposed to the game or thought of it as a foreign novelty like soccer. For another thing, until recently hockey players were tremendously dedicated men who played more for love than for money and were therefore not vulnerable to corrupting influences. And without corruptible players, gamblers don't have that edge so necessary to guarantee a big killing. So they left hockey alone.

"'Then, in 1967, came expansion. First, expansion of the NHL, then a few years later establishment of the World Hockey League. The expansion has been fast and turbulent and has radically changed the face of the sport, as I've stated earlier. The biggest changes, which are tied together, are that it has become more of an American sport and that it has unleashed huge amounts of capital. Franchises have been established or are being set up in almost every major city or region, even unlikely warm-weather ones like Atlanta, Miami, and Charleston. Even more important, though, the salary and bonus war triggered by this expansion has spoiled the haves and made the have-nots greedy and jealous. When such a situation exists, the way is opened to bribes, fixes, and other forms of corruption.

"'In this chapter I will not only elaborate on these contentions but reveal the details of a gambling scandal, hitherto unknown except to a handful of individuals, that could blow the sport right off the ice.'"

Ellen fitted the outline over the rest of the script, tamped the pages down until they were neatly aligned, and replaced them in the folder. She took a sip of wine, a puff of her little cigar, and studied me over the rim of her glass. I sensed she was not merely looking at me for my reaction but examining me as a man.

What she saw was a tall, athletic-looking guy in his mid-thirties, wearing a camelhair blazer over an open-collared brown shirt, who possessed an open face that, save one or two anomalous features, might be characterized as interesting or attractive or, if you were sufficiently infatuated or drunk or stoned, handsome. The anomalies included a war-weary nose, veteran of numberless campaigns on high school, college, military, and professional football fields, and tightly curled ochre hair that, left to its own devices, would flourish into a splendid blond natural. This is the product of a suspected liaison between one of my ancestors and a slave girl. I figure I'm one thirty-second black which makes me a something-oroon. Except for a somewhat swarthy complexion, there is no other physical resemblance to my distant African forebears but there is something impalpable circulating in my lymphatic system that gives me an odd affinity to black people; it has not endeared me to some of the redder-necked specimens of the white race I grew up with.

But what Ellen Boudreau was scrutinizing particularly was my eyes, in which mingled my personal and professional interest in her. "A gambling scandal that could blow the sport right off the ice," I repeated. "That's pretty heavy."

This rather fatuous observation was greeted by the silence it deserved. The atmosphere in the room suddenly turned thick with trouble, like the ozone-filled air in a generating plant, and I knew we were coming to the heart of the problem. I closed my eyes and groped for the answer. It came to me a moment later. "The rest of the script is missing, isn't it?"

"Yes," Ellen said. "It's missing."

"Whoo boy." I let it sink in a minute. "How do you know it's missing?"

"About a week before he died," Ellen said, "I called Guy to ask him how the book was coming along. He said he had most of it in rough form and was waiting till the end of the season to finish it and type a final draft."

"And this gambling scandal he outlined, you think he'd have completed it at the time of his death?"

"At the rate he was writing, I'm positive of it."

I closed my eyes again and formed a picture of this script floating around somewhere like a half-submerged landmine waiting to go off. Of course, it might never go off. "How do you know it wasn't destroyed? Don't you think the same person or people who killed Laclede found the script and destroyed it?"

"That's a possibility," Sturdevant answered with a flutter of the eyes, "but by no means a certainty."

"I assume you've looked for it."

Ellen nodded. "Right after I learned of Guy's death, I called Buzzy Chambers and told him Guy had been writing the book."

Buzzy picked up the thread. "As soon as it was discreet to do so, I visited Guy's widow. We searched the house thoroughly but couldn't find a trace of the script. We don't know if he hid it, burned it, or, as you say, if it was appropriated by whoever murdered him. We don't even know if the person who murdered him is the same one who took the script. Hell, Dave, we don't even know for sure if he was murdered."

I shook my head and sighed. "You sure have narrowed the thing down."

"It's not quite as bleak as all that," Buzzy tried to reassure me. "You have a lot of leads, maybe even the answers, right here in the completed chapters. It's a matter of tracking them down."

"Your best bet," Vince Sturdevant said, "is to read the manuscript. Then we can sit down and hash it over and draw up some sort of strategy for an investigation."

"It sounds," I said, "about as easy as discovering who passed wind in the Cotton Bowl on New Year's Day," I said.

Ellen Boudreau frowned at the vulgar reference, but I didn't care. I had just seen my dream of a playoff-saturated April vacation go up in smoke and I was mad.

CHAPTER II

· · · ·

Ellen and I stepped onto the elevator and rode down silently together, facing the front of the car like strangers. The
chrome doors parted and we walked side by side through
the lobby and out into Dominion Square, a beautiful park
bordered by the imposing Imperial Bank of Commerce
Building, the Windsor Hotel, the Dominion Square Building
and, behind us, the Sun Life Building. Children played tag
around statues of Laurier, Burns, and the mandatory one
of Queen Victoria. The cool air was bracing and the chirp
of birds recently liberated from the throes of winter almost
intoxicating. It was inconceivable that Ellen could go her
way and I mine, yet I felt oddly diffident, not because of any
innate shyness, in which I'm notoriously lacking in the presence of a handsome woman, but because Ellen radiated an
intimidating indifference that surrounded her like a shield.

I resorted to a tired gambit and crossed my fingers. "I'm
starved. Have you had lunch?"

"No."

"Will you join me?"

"What time is it?"

I looked at my watch. "One-fifteen. Do you have to be somewhere?"

"Not at any precise time. I'd like to drop by the Forum sometime this afternoon, though."

"The Forum?"

"Yes. The Buffalo Sabres play the Canadiens tonight. The Sabres will be practicing this afternoon. My...I know someone on the team."

I felt a sensation of disappointment at the mention of the possessive pronoun. Her what? Boyfriend? Fiancé? Maybe, hopefully, brother. Suddenly a bell rang, and I clapped my head for being so stupid. "Boudreau—are you related to Ned Boudreau?" Ned was the Sabres' goalie.

"He's my...husband."

"You pause as if you're not sure."

"You inquire as if you had a right to," she answered sharply, flustering me. I started gushing apologies but she finally touched my arm and said, "I'm sorry. Ned and I are separated. I'm a little touchy on the subject."

"That's okay. I have one or two touchies in my personal life myself."

"Forget it. I'd be delighted to have lunch with you. Are you an adventurous diner or a typical Texan?"

"I've been known to eat a few other things besides steak and eggs and home fries," I said. It was hard to tell whether she was teasing me or had really written me off as a stereotype. If the latter, she wouldn't be the first. "Typical Texan" is a convenient cloak for me. It makes people underestimate me and drop their guard. Still, the remark stung me a little.

"Do you know Vieux Montréal?"

"Not really. This is only my second or third time here."

"I know a restaurant I think you'll like." She linked her arm in mine and we strolled to St. Antoine, bore left and continued along St. Antoine until we reached McGill, which marks the boundary between Old Montreal and its modern counterpart. Entering the ancient quarter was like emerging from a rapids into a quiet, limpid lake, and Ellen slowed our pace to point out a few highlights of the charming city within the city. I must confess to less than total appreciation, however. Not that Bon-Secours Chapel and the Chateau de Ramezy and Notre Dame Church and Les Messieurs de St.-Sulpice and all the wonderful old commercial houses and monuments weren't enchanting, but the realization that Ellen was Ned Boudreau's wife—or estranged wife, I guess was the proper term—had preempted my curiosity. I was about to indulge it with a carefully phrased question when we turned up Rue St. Paul and ducked into a dim restaurant so small and obscure you'd run right past it without a knowledgeable guide. It had no more than a dozen tables, but almost all were filled. Ellen said something in French to the proprietor and he seated us in a corner under a grimy mural depicting some unfamiliar episode in Canadian history. I ordered a demi of Chablis and some menus but Ellen said, "I've already ordered our lunch. I'm sure you'll be pleased."

She took her pack of Winchesters out of her purse and offered me one. I took it, lit us both up and looked around, fishing for something to say to break the ice. I was relieved when Ellen took the initiative. "I'm sorry, I thought you knew that Ned was my husband. I'd assumed Vince Sturdevant briefed you before you came up to Montreal."

"No, he didn't tell me anything about anything. But of course, now I understand how you knew Guy Laclede. Guy and Ned were the goalies for Chicago for…what? Three years?"

"Four. It was Guy's wife Babette who introduced me to Ned. I'd had a crush on Ned for the longest time. We married in Ned's second year at Chicago. The four of us—Ned and I, Guy and Babette—were very tight friends until…"She stopped herself. "We were inseparable."

"Until that fatal playoff series with the Rangers."

"Yes," she said wistfully, "that fatal series. Fatal in more ways than one."

She left the thought hanging but I paused before reaching for it. "You rapped my knuckles before for prying."

She shrugged. "Oh well, I don't mind talking about it now, really. It's all water over the dam."

"Is it?"

She flinched a little as if I'd caught her in a lie. "You mean, if it's finished, why am I going to see Ned this afternoon? Well, we're still friends, you see."

"Yes," I said sympathetically, "I know a thing or two about the friendship phase." My mind was flashing the breadth of a continent to my ex-wife Nancy in Houston. At the drop of a hat, I was prepared to talk about it.

But Ellen was too involved in her own sad memories. "You know of course what happened after that series."

"Sure. The fans were so mad at the team they forced the management to can the coach and get rid of Guy and your husband. It was outrageous."

"I'm glad you think so. I mean, the Stanley Cup meant a lot to Chicago since the Black Hawks hadn't won it since 1961. But to punish Ned and Guy and Coach Staley, to make them scapegoats that way…" Even in the faint light of the restaurant, I could see two red spots rush to Ellen's cheeks as her indignation flamed. "It was a political thing," she said. "Mayor Daley got a hand in it—oh, it was just the worst." She smashed the stub of her little cigar in the ashtray and scowled.

The proprietor brought out our wine and an endive salad.

"Ned was so bitter he retired but that just made him morbid and bored and impossible to live with. After a year. the Sabres approached him and he signed up with them and we moved to Buffalo. Buffalo," she said with a face.

"You couldn't hack Buffalo," I said, having spent a few days in that town.

"No, it wasn't my kind of city. We quarreled and quarreled until I couldn't stand it anymore. I'd thought Ned's spirit would brighten to be playing again but the Chicago experience had just warped him. It was like someone had thrown acid on his face and scarred him for life. Anyway, I left him and went to New York. I used some connections to get a job with Streeter and here I am."

"Here you are indeed. I'll drink to that."

We clinked glasses and burrowed into our salads, which were followed by a côte de veau I'd have to describe as sublime. We talked aimlessly, mostly about hockey, but as we were having coffee she said, "Are you separated, too, Mr. Bolt?"

My eyebrows shot up. "Divorced. How did you know?"

"You've alluded to it indirectly."

"I didn't think you'd heard."

"I'm not that wrapped up in myself, am I?" she said apologetically and for the first time, her features softened into something resembling vulnerable femininity.

"You're wrapped up in something, I can't figure out what," I said. I told her about how I'd broken up with Nancy after I was injured playing for the Dallas Cowboys. Larry Wilson of the St. Louis Cardinals had ripped up my ankles on a tackle in my third season as tight end, but instead of rehabilitating myself, I succumbed to the Bolt clan's dynastic tradition of pickling our self-pity in alcohol. By the time my nightmare ended two years later, all I had was the shirt on my back and a divorce decree somebody had slapped in my hand while I was sleeping one off.

Ellen talked some more about Ned, about the good times before everything had gone blooey, and I could see that whatever she might say, the water had not completely flowed over the dam of her marriage. There was still pain and sorrow and tenderness and the lingering hope of reconciliation, just as there was for me whenever I thought about Nancy or visited her and our daughter Jody. But I selfishly hoped there would be no reconciliation for Ned and Ellen and my pulse quickened when she said, "Would you care to escort me to the game tonight?"

"Nothing could make me happier," I said.

We taxied to her hotel, Le Chateau Champlain on Place du Canada, then I walked from there to my hotel, the Bonaventure on de la Gauchetièrre. The contrast between the breathtaking modernity of the Bonaventure and the mellow antiquity of the old section it overlooked was awesome. Beyond Ville-Marie the view from my high window embraced the St. Lawrence and the sister islands of Notre-Dame and Sainte-Helene, where some permanent structures held over from Expo 70 could still be seen.

Reluctantly turning my back to this scene, I settled into a comfortable armchair with Guy Laclede's unfinished book in my lap, lit a Romeo y Julieta panatella (as Cuban cigars are not outlawed in Canada, I usually indulge my passion for them to the point of illness whenever I cross the border), and began reading.

It didn't take me long to get into the book and, after a few pages, to get completely absorbed. It wasn't that the stuff I read was completely new to me as an insider in the sports world I was familiar with many of the seamy aspects of hockey that Guy Laclede had set out to expose. Sexual misconduct, brawling, ugly French-English rivalries and discrimination (the equivalent of the black problem in the United States), petty gambling, drug abuse—with minor variations these are all standard equipment in every professional sport, and hockey was not exempt.

What gripped me was the lusty fervor of Laclede's attack, the almost gleeful way he applied scalpel, lance, and hatchet, and the vindictive manner in which he named names. Though the typing was sloppy and failed with errors, typeovers, and penciled changes, the style itself was clear and incisive and amazingly refined. Unlike so many hockey players who are sucked out of school as soon as they reach the minimum draft age of twenty, Laclede's father, Ellen had told me, had insisted he complete his college education and it showed. He had brought to his task a full bag of literary devices ranging from scorn, sarcasm, and bombast to cool analysis and statistical support. If you wanted to rip the lid off professional hockey, you couldn't have picked a better man.

Yet the impression that remained with me, after I set the script down, was that this had been not merely a mercenary undertaking for Laclede but a labor of love. Or more accurately, a labor of hate, as if he was getting back at hockey for some mortal hurt it had done to him. Admittedly he had been dealt with shabbily in the Chicago episode, admittedly, too, with a few breaks he might have gone on to be a fine goalie on a "dynasty" team, which Chicago had promised to be until the canning of coach and goalies had plunged it into the mire of mediocrity. But that didn't explain his unnatural bitterness. He seemed determined, with his book, to pull the whole hockey establishment to doom with him. When I came to that passage in the outline promising the revelation of a gambling scandal that could "blow the sport off the ice," I felt a tremor of fear in my guts, for I knew now that this was no idle boast. I threw the script onto the floor as if it bore contagion. I actually felt unclean and took a shower, then napped for an hour. I dozed restlessly. A battalion of grotesque hockey phantoms swept past me as if I were a goaltender fighting off a barrage of explosive missiles. I was drenched in sweat when I woke and had to take another shower.

I dressed, studied the menu on my dresser, but decided I wasn't that hungry and would dine later or grab something at the Forum. Besides, it was almost time to pick Ellen up. That prospect excited me in a way nothing had excited me in a long time.

I walked to the Chateau Champlain and announced myself on the house phone. Ellen came downstairs promptly, dressed in a tweedy skirt and tight sweater that displayed her figure to far more effect than the clothes she'd worn earlier in the day. Her breasts were small and high, her waist narrow, her hips round but not large, and her legs beautifully muscled and smooth. She wore a bright red scarf around her neck that set off her black hair like fire in the night. Her perfume was subtle and arousing and, being a normally vain male, I couldn't help feeling I was the object of the special care she'd taken to make herself attractive.

The picture was spoiled a little by a vaguely distracted expression on her face and I suspected she'd had an upsetting confrontation with her husband this afternoon. "How do the Sabres look for tonight?" I asked, veiling my real question behind an innocuous one.

But she veiled her answer as well. "They're up for the game. They're out of contention, of course, but they want to spoil it for Montreal. If they win tonight, they'll knock the Canadiens out of second place."

"Should be interesting," I muttered.

I started to hail a taxi but she said, "No, the Metro is faster and cheaper. We have a station right here."

We descended into the bright, clean, beautiful modern miracle that is the Montreal subway and rode in eerie, rubber-wheeled silence to Westmount Square, from which it was a short walk to the Forum. As we glided along, I ventured a remark about Guy Laclede's book but she put her finger over her lips. "Unlike New York's subway system, anything you say on a Montreal train can be overheard at the other end of the car. Why don't we save it till later?"

I laughed. "You're right. They ought to bill this as the subway that lets you think. As a matter of fact, the ride is so quiet I can hear you thinking, too."

"Can you?"

"Uh-huh."

"What do you hear?"

"I hear you thinking you're kind of glad to be with me."

"That's somewhat conceited but not inaccurate."

"If I can wade through your syntax, I gather that means yes."

"Yes, it means yes."

"Glad enough not to take offense if I ask you a personal question?"

"Don't push your luck," she said, playfully but seriously. Then, as changeable as mountain weather, she said, "I suppose you're curious about how it went with Ned this afternoon."

"Well, it's none of my—"

"I didn't see him."

"You didn't?"

"That is, I saw him but he didn't see me. I just watched the practice and left."

"Lost your courage?"

"Yes. But I was also afraid of making him uptight before a game."

"So you've decided to make him uptight after the game."

"I thought I might just drop by for a few minutes, yes. If that's all right with you."

I laughed again. "All right with me? He's your husband, for crying out loud!"

She didn't laugh but the humor of it did manage to put a pretty crease on the corner of her mouth. "That's right, he is, isn't he?"

We pulled into Westmount Square and shuffled onto the platform with the tide of fans that had gradually filled the train and I felt a glow of optimism as we approached the gates of the stadium. Ellen must, I thought, be interested enough in me to think of me as a rival to Ned. Otherwise, why would she ask my permission to see him?

In spite of the fact that the Canadiens had already locked up a playoff berth and the Sabres were in the cellar of the Adams Division of the NHL, the Forum was still jammed to the rafters with the most discriminating and vociferous hockey fans on this or any other continent. Though the official capacity of the stadium is 16,500 sittees and another 2000 standees, the fans are on their feet so much I doubt if anyone would notice if they removed all the seats completely.

From the concerted oohs and ahs that greeted us as we passed through the lobby, I gathered that the action had already begun. Ellen said something to an usher at the top of the stairs leading to the center section box seats and he nodded and led us down to the President's box behind the glass at center ice. "You're amazing," I shouted at her. "Every time you whisper something to someone in this city, things happen."

"Mr. Sturdevant put his seats at my disposal," she said with a smile. We slid into the box and I found myself awash in a sea of VIPs—league officials, Montreal and

Buffalo brass, and some visiting firemen. I identified or shook hands with Bruce Norris, Chairman of the Board of the NHL and owner of the Detroit Red Wings, ex-president of the NHL Clarence Campbell, Sam Pollock, Jean Belliveau and "Toe" Blake, all Montreal Canadiens execs, and Jack Kent Cooke visiting from Los Angeles. Many of them greeted Ellen by first name and her stock—which was already blue-chip in my portfolio—rose precipitously and split two-for-one.

"You sure are popular around here," I said.

"I told you, I'm a hockey nut. I'm one of the few women to contribute to the Hockey News and not get laughed out of Canada."

She leaned forward and put her chin in her hands and immediately lost herself in the action. We'd missed about three minutes, but there'd been no score, and the next ten consisted of desultory sparring about which I didn't see much to get excited. But Ellen picked up nuances that made me realize how little I understood the game. She alternately cheered, groaned, muttered, and commented with the expertise of a laddie doing color commentary in a broadcasting booth. "Watch Larue and Markovich switch wings next time the Sabres attack," she urged me, sending me burrowing into my program for their numbers. "God, that rookie Bennett has moves! Did you see that deke? And he's American, too. Oh, come on, Frank, you can skate better than that! The bloody fool has lead in his cup! Hey, Irv, watch Masson's high stick! Worst buggering referee in the league, that one is."

About two-thirds of the way through the first period, the game heated up. The Canadiens flowed around the Sabre net like the Blue Angels in precision formation, firing, recovering, rebounding, passing out, re-forming, and peeling off for another rush, chasing the puck to the boards, digging it out, checking and pressing in an exhibition of the kind of control that had made them the jewels in the NHL's crown over the decades. The Sabres, in desperation, could only bat the puck blindly out of the zone but this did no good except to give them a moment's breather before the Canadiens swarmed again or an icing call required a faceoff in Sabre territory. In fact, it was off such a faceoff that the Habs scored their first goal, a screaming screened slap shot by the aging but invincible veteran, Yvon Cornoyer.

"Shit," Ellen groaned, biting her lip. "Ned never could handle those low ones to his stick side."

I looked at the masked Sabre goalie leaning disgustedly against the frame of his net and suddenly remembered he was Ellen's husband. There was something in the tone of her criticism that was very much like a wife revealing an intimate secret about her husband—"He could never close his collar button by himself," or "He was always getting his sleeves in the gravy when he ate." I gazed at the lonely figure, heavy and clumsy-looking in his well-padded blue, gold, and white uniform, and wondered about the man under the gear and mask, wondered what it was about him that drew Ellen morbidly back to him in spite of the shitty end of the stick he'd handed her. I felt another wave of jealousy and possessiveness and hoped the Canadiens humiliated him tonight.

But he kept cool and hung in. The Canadiens relaxed after bounding into the lead and the action shifted to the other end of the ice. The Sabres got aggressive and forced Edgar Masson to high stick a Sabre attacker. This time, to Ellen's satisfaction, Referee Irv Landon called Masson on it, precipitating a power-play. The Sabres capitalized on it, converting the six-on-five situation into a goal with a faked pass and super wrist-shot by Markovich. A moment later the green light and siren brought the first period to a conclusion. The fans applauded. They'd seen some good hockey.

Ellen led me to a private lounge for VIPs not far from where we were sitting. A punch bowl, some hors d'oeuvres and a cheese board were set up along a wall underneath a row of portraits of NHL founding fathers and hockey greats. I'd gotten a little hungry and consumed half a dozen smoked salmon on rye toasts, washing them down with a cup of mellow red punch. Ellen must have waved at two dozen bigwigs but declined to engage any in conversation, preferring instead to hold me to an isolated corner of the lounge. A moment later I understood why. "You haven't told me what you thought of the manuscript," she said in a low voice.

"It's strong stuff," I said, matching her conspiratorial tone. "Is that true about drug use? I hadn't realized it had made that much headway in hockey."

"Another symptom of the malade Américaine," she sighed.

"Do you think Joey Forbes might be involved in Guy's death? I mean, he couldn't have been very happy to learn he was described in a forthcoming book as a speed freak."

"If he knew he was described in a forthcoming book," she corrected me. "And that, Dave, is for you to find out." She handed her cup to me for a refill. I went to the punch bowl and ladled out another portion, smiling smugly to myself as I realized she'd addressed me by my first name. I returned and she sipped half of it down, then pulled a Winchester out of her purse. I lit it briskly. "The same is true," she said, "of Chub Zaretski, Ed Boniface, Guy Rameau, Mark Ryan, Teddy Lancaster—and of course, Jean-Philippe Boileau. They all had a reason to see Guy's mouth gagged or his book suppressed or worse. But if they didn't know Guy was writing a book about their sins—well, then, that eliminates them. Every charge Guy leveled in those pages is also a charge of high explosive. With his career on the line, any man mentioned in the book becomes a potential murderer. You've no choice but to grill each and every one."

"That's not asking too much," I said sarcastically.

"What narrows it down is, I'm sure most of them weren't aware Guy knew what he knew or was writing a book. So, when you speak to them, if they express genuine surprise, you can strike them off the list."

"How am I supposed to distinguish between genuine surprise and the fake variety?"

"You'll have to rely on your instincts, I imagine," she said. "By the same token, if your instincts tell you one of these guys is playing it cagey, then he may be the one we're looking for. But of course," she added with a pout, "I still think the one we're looking for doesn't appear in the chapters you read. He's in the ones that disappeared."

"It's going to be hard to start this job without a defeatist attitude," I said as the chimes sounded signifying the teams had taken the ice for their second-period warmup.

"I know what you mean," Ellen said, her eyes mirroring my own sense of futility. "It's like looking for a typo in the New Yorker magazine."

"I've never seen one," I said.

"Exactly." She sighed and clicked her tongue empathetically. Then she touched a napkin to my lapel to absorb a drop of punch that had fallen off my cup. "But somehow, I think that if anyone can do it, you can."

Between the solicitous gesture and the inspiring remark, I felt like a soldier singled out by a reviewing general before a battle and told the destiny of the engagement depended on him. He knows it's pure bullshit, yet when the flares light up the sky, his figure leads the charge across no-man's land.

We returned to our seats.

The next twenty minutes of hockey were breathtaking. I don't know what coach Joe Crozier told his Sabres in the locker room but they swarmed over the Canadiens like crazed hornets. Three-quarters of the action took place on Canadien ice. The young but aggressive Sabre line kept Montreal goalie Ken Dryden busier than the proverbial one-armed paperhanger with fleas. They took nineteen shots on goal as against four for the Habs and two of those nineteen triggered the red light. The hitting was tremendous and at times vicious. Not only did the Sabres not seem to care if they drew penalties, they fought harder when one of their number was in the penalty box and inflicted the ultimate insult on Montreal by scoring a shorthanded goal on a daring steal by Larue and a breakaway that left Dryden sprawled in front of his net like a big rag-doll tossed over a child's shoulder.

The Canadiens looked bewildered and gun-shy as they skated off the ice at the end of the second period. The fans booed lustily, which enraged Ellen because that made it look as if the Canadiens could have played better. I don't think any team could have withstood that fusillade.

But whatever had ignited the Sabres in the second period fizzled in the third. The sign of a veteran team is that it knows how to pace itself and Montreal is nothing if not a veteran team. The Canadiens' attack wasn't quite as frenzied as the Sabres' had been the previous period but it was intense and determined and the Canadiens came out popping. The grunts and winces were audible above the thunderous shouting of the fans and whenever a Canadien checked a Sabre into the boards in front of us, I involuntarily shielded my face from what I was certain would be a shower of shattered glass.

Now Ned Boudreau became the harried defender and there was one sequence of half a dozen shots in the space of a minute when I did not believe he could hold out. Yet he made save after miraculous save, his arms and legs darting out like a man in the last spasms of his death rattle. Out of the corner of my eye, I watched Ellen. She jumped out of her seat with each close call, arms and legs twitching in sympathy with her husband's as if her body language-could stop the puck. Her lusty cheers for Buffalo attracted baleful glares from the Montreal rooters surrounding us but partisan though he may be, the Montreal fan is above all a connoisseur of hockey. Thus at the end of the barrage, as Boudreau uncrumpled his body to reveal the puck trapped beneath his hip, the crowd gave him a standing ovation.

He wasn't so lucky on a second flurry of shots on goal late in the third period and finally succumbed to a nifty Cornoyer backhand rebound that soared into the upper corner of the net like a golf ball coming off a three-iron. Still, he managed to cling to his 3-2 lead and the Sabres clinched it in the last minute when, Montreal pulling Dryden for a sixth attacker, a rookie wing named Selig smacked an open-net goal from the Canadien blue line.

The green light had no sooner flashed than Ned Boudreau tore off his mask as if it had been suffocating him. He was bathed in glistening sweat and gulped air with great tormented heaves as his teammates hugged him and mussed his abundant straw-colored hair. I'd seen his picture years ago when he was with Chicago and more recently on television but never this close up. He was a handsome man despite the black gap in his front teeth. He had a ruddy, outdoorsy complexion drawn tightly over high cheekbones and a belligerently outthrust jaw. His nose was battered and asymmetrical and added to the almost classic profile of a rugged and formidable athlete, an archetypal gladiator. Only his limpid blue eyes and the hint of a crooked little smile took the edge off it and suggested virtues such as tenderness or a sense of humor that redeemed an otherwise cruel face.

"Do you still want to see him?" I asked Ellen.

She hesitated. "Yes, I suppose so. Will you come with me?"

Now it was I who hesitated. "Well, I sure would like to shake that man's hand."

"He did put in a good game, didn't he? Except for that first goal. I told him a thousand times to work on that weakness but he was lazy."

"I'd hate to be a goalie married to you," I said, guiding her into the tunnel deep in the bowels of the arena.

"Yes, in that respect I was not a good wife. I knew too much and I couldn't keep my mouth shut. But it was for his own good even if it sounded like nagging. In any case, I committed no other sin against him and I've acquitted myself."

"For the breakup, you mean."

"Yes. In the end, it was his fault. I could have stayed with him, even..." She swallowed the qualifying phrase and I'm sure the one she ultimately used was a substitute. "Even in Buffalo. Yes, I could have stayed with him even in Buffalo if he hadn't become so damned bitter, so mean. But he was simply impossible. He struck me on several occasions and once I thought he was going to kill me. And that was it for me."

"Yes," I said, "that's when my wife cleared out of my own marriage, too. What is it about women, just because we blacken their eyes or knock their noses out of kilter, they feel they have to leave us?"

"Vanity, I suppose," Ellen answered, smiling sardonically. "Bruises and lacerations ruin our makeup."

We plunged into a maze of corridors and were swept up in an eddy of boisterous fans, mostly kids, rushing to the

Montreal locker room in hopes of glimpsing some of their heroes. The tunnel forked and we veered off in the direction of the visitors' locker room. The traffic thinned out to a trickle, our heels clacking hollowly as we negotiated the oval. There was a small knot of Sabres fans, reporters, and curiosity-seekers milling around outside the heavy steel door, jostling a harried-looking guard with a squawking walkie-talkie hooked to a shoulder strap.

Just beyond this clot of people, where the tunnel bent off into the backstretch of the arena's oval, I noticed the glare of white floodlights and guessed that someone was being interviewed for television. "I reckon that'll be your husband," I said, placing my hand on Ellen's waist and steering her through the shoal of humanity. "If anyone deserves the game ball, or whatever they call it in hockey, he's the one."

We shouldered through half a dozen more rooters, stepped over some cables, and stopped at the perimeter of a roped-off zone surrounding a little platform. Upon it stood Ned Boudreau, leaning away from a mike held by a wild-haired dude in horn-rimmed glasses and outsized blazer who looked like a plump Woody Allen. Boudreau loomed big and bulky on the platform, like a padded dummy used for target practice. He carried stick, glove, and mask under his arm and yanked them several times out of the clutches of children reaching across the rope to touch them. His hair hung limply around his face as if someone had just dumped a bucket of water on his head. He'd put his bridge back in his mouth for the folks at home and looked even more handsome but also crueler up close than he'd looked at the end of the game. I felt another twinge of jealousy as well as puzzlement that Ellen could have been content for so long with a man who was so obviously a prick.

I turned to Ellen. Her face registered opposing emotions of joy and fear and I suddenly regretted deeply my decision to accompany her down here. "I think maybe I'll wait outside," I said, pulling away.

"No, please don't." She put her hand on my arm as if for support.

It was just my luck that Ned Boudreau chose that moment to scan the crowd for familiar faces and found Ellen's. He stopped in the middle of a sentence and his expression, like a traffic light, flashed in rapid succession from green for gladness, yellow for suspicion, and red for displeasure as he noticed her tugging my arm. He shook his head in bewilderment as he tried to remember what he had been saying to the interviewer. Finally, he muttered a reply still glaring at Ellen. A moment later the interview ended and the floodlights died as if shot out with pistols, plunging the tunnel momentarily into darkness until our eyes adjusted to the sixty-watt dimness of the overhead globes.

My vision finally achieved parity with the light level and I observed Ned Boudreau lumbering off the platform on his skates and onto the rubber mat outside the locker room door. He gazed at Ellen with a combination of anger and diffidence. "Hello, Ellen." He possessed a mellow tenor voice that quavered slightly. I couldn't tell if that was due to exhaustion from the game, nervousness from the television interview, or surprise to see Ellen. "What brings you to Montreal?" He darted a glance at me.

"Just an assignment from my publisher. You played very well tonight."

"Their first score—I bet I know what you must have been thinking."

I felt a lump in my throat. This was the kind of intimate connubial exchange to which outsiders shouldn't be privy.

I started to fade out of the picture when Boudreau fixed me with a penetrating gaze.

Ellen snapped her fingers. "Oh, I'm sorry. Ned, I'd like you to meet Dave Bolt."

I offered my hand but he just glared at me, speculating about my relationship with Ellen and, perhaps, sizing me up as a potential antagonist. He could not have been too well pacified by Ellen's explanation. "Dave is a players' agent. He's up here from New York on business, too."

"How convenient. And I'll bet you're staying at the same hotel, too."

"As a matter of fact, we're not," she said patiently but with reddening cheeks. I didn't care much for his sneering reference and stepped forward but Ellen put a hand on my arm, the second such gesture Boudreau had seen in the space of a couple of minutes.

Taking my cue from Ellen, I said, "I just met your wife this morning." I emphasized the "your wife" and flashed an affable if strained smile.

"Sure you did," he said, giving a horrible laugh. Then he thrust out his jaw at Ellen and said, "Why don't you cut the bullshit! I wasn't born yesterday, you know."

Ellen ran a nervous hand through her hair. "Ned, it's nothing like that. Dave and I are—"

"It's bad enough you left me but to come down here flaunting your boyfriend…"

I started to get a little bugged. True, I had designs on Ellen or at least some healthy fantasies but it was still a mighty leap from thought to deed and she had given me not the slightest bit of encouragement. What made this scene particularly bad was the presence of fans and reporters, who began to press around us, attracted by the hostility. I suppose I should have walked away but I didn't care for the slur for Ellen's sake, especially in public. "Hey, friend," I said to Boudreau quietly, "don't you think you're being a little hasty?"

He poked a finger sharply into my sternum. "Lemme tell you something, mister. You better fuck off while I'm still in a good mood."

"This is what you call a good mood?" I laughed. I sized up both him and the situation and all precincts cast votes instantly against belligerence. In stature and weight, Boudreau and I were about equal but he was padded from the shoulders down and was armed with a hockey stick. He also still had his skates on, which could cut a deeper tread in me than a snow tire if he decided to drop Marquess of Queensbury rules and come out kicking. But an even more forceful consideration was the publicity. With reporters taking notes and cameramen adjusting their f-stops and shutter speeds to capture this moment for posterity, that low, anonymous profile for which I'd been selected for Vince Sturdevant's investigation would be blown and my mission destroyed before it even got underway.

My daddy taught me contradictory lessons about fighting, which I alternately called into play according to whether or not I thought I could lick my opponent. One was, Never Back Down. The other was, Discretion Is the Better Part of Valor. I was about to opt for the latter when someone, I never did see who or determine whether it was accidental or stupidly intentional, nudged me from the back.

Ned, of course, mistook this for a declaration of war but before I had a chance to apologize he'd brought the flat of his stick, which was nestled in the crook of his left arm, around with the same quickness that had stopped thirty-five shots on goal earlier in the evening. I heard the stick whiz through the air and caught sight of the blur of black tape on the blade but I'd have had to have the reflexes of a bluebottle fly to evade that blazing slap shot. The blade caught me on the cheek and ear and a phosphorus shell of blue twinkles ignited the dimness of the tunnel, while a high-pitched ringing triggered in my head that was not to subside for an hour. My knees went syrupy but I grabbed Boudreau's jersey as I went down and yanked him on top of me. His left arm, still clutching all his gear, was momentarily immobilized, and I took advantage of it with a pounding right cross to his temple. He fell heavily on top of me and I grappled for his free right hand. I captured his wrist and held it close to his side so he couldn't impart much momentum to a swing. That was good thinking—if one's opponent is a gentleman and not a man to whom brawling is as natural as breathing.

He butted my nose with his head.

Then he raked my shin with his skate.

Then he bit my shoulder.

I felt the ugly, sour taste of blood draining into my throat from my nose, heard a loud keening in my ear, and felt pain in four places at once. Pretty obviously, I was getting the worst of it. My only retaliation was to bring my knee up between his legs with everything I had and believe me, cup or no cup, that has to ring some bells! Boudreau let out a bull-like groan and for a moment his thrashing stopped.

Words fail to convey my relief at the sight of the security cop, three of Boudreau's teammates, and a baker's dozen of private citizens locking Boudreau in their hands and pulling him off me. He continued flailing and even when they pinned him to the wall, he managed to clip one of his Sabres friends on the jaw.

"You better get out of here, mister," the guard said pointing to an exit. Ellen stood flattened against one wall, tears streaming down her cheeks. She stepped up to me, looked at her husband, shook her head in pity, and helped the guard usher me out of the tunnel. Even as the heavy door slammed behind us I could hear Boudreau's curses.

Ellen hailed a taxi and with the help of the driver, a funny little man with a walrus mustache who I think mistook me for a Buffalo Sabre, eased me into the back seat. The driver shook his fist at me and said something in French about Buffalo.

Still in tears, Ellen delved into her purse and pulled out a little packet of Kleenex and pressed the tissues to my nostrils. "Oh Dave, I'm so sorry."

"How's that?"

"I said I'm sorry."

"You'll have to speak up. I got more sirens going for me than London in the blitz."

"Do you want to go to a doctor?" she shouted.

"No, just take me back to my hotel." She directed the driver to the Bonaventure. "Christ, I knew I shouldn't have gone down there with you."

"Maybe it's all for the best," she said.

Despite the acrid taste of blood in my mouth, I found this remark funny and had to laugh. "That's easy for you to say!"

"I had to find out if he'd changed," she said, mostly to herself.

"Twenty stitches in my shin says he hasn't."

"Let me see." She lifted my foot up and peered at it in the intermittent streetlights along St. Antoine. "It's a bad scrape, but I don't think it goes very deep." She placed my foot in her lap and dabbed the blood off with some more tissues.

Though I felt like I'd just been sucked through a turboprop, I realized that my injuries weren't as serious as they must have seemed to Ellen, whose guilt magnified them. The soothing caress of her hand along my leg inspired the rather unchivalrous idea of using them to strengthen my bond with her.

"Would you mind helping me up to my room?" I said as we pulled up to the hotel. "I'm going to need a little first aid."

"Oh no, not at all."

We fetched a few hundred stares as I limped through the Bonaventure leaning heavily on Ellen. A host of solicitous porters and guests offered aid but Ellen waved them off.

We elevatored to my room, where we examined my wounds with great clucks of concern. The fact is that in my Dallas Cowboys days, I routinely walked off a football field with more bruises than I'd received at the hands of Ned Boudreau. But why let Ellen know that? My shin bore an ugly but superficial skinning along the tibia; my temple and cheekbone had an angry red egg where Boudreau had whacked me with his stick; my shoulder had a couple of deep purple blood clots where he'd bit me, and my nose made a funny clicking sound when I pinched the cartilage, indicating a separation—a condition I was so used to it was hardly worth mentioning. All in all, I'd taken a good beating but nothing that wouldn't repair itself in a few days' time. The worst effects would show up tomorrow when the black-and-blue mice showed up under my eyes. A pair of dark glasses would take care of that.

"Shall I call for the doctor?" Ellen said, surveying the damage with a sigh.

"No, for room service. Double bourbon for me and see if they have branch water."

I went into the bathroom and stripped out of my blood-spattered clothes. My blazer would have to go to the cleaners, the shirt was torn where Boudreau's teeth had penetrated, and the pants, shredded from knee to cuff, were beyond salvation. I threw them in the wastebasket and stepped into the shower. The hot water stung, then soothed me. When I climbed out I realized the ringing in my ears had subsided to a low-pitched whistle. I blotted the tenderer areas of my body, then wrapped a towel around my butt and opened the door.

Ellen, just finishing a phone call, appraised my physique with the coolness of a woman accustomed to athletes' bodies and I got the impression I scored high marks in her book. Except for a couple of years in which I let my flesh go to pot—the same pot as my soul, after I left Nancy and conducted my survey of grogshops of the American Southwest—I've kept myself in good condition with regular workouts, weightlifting, jogging, and scrimmages in whatever sport happens to be in season.

Ellen glanced clinically at the bulge under my towel and shifted her eyes uncomfortably elsewhere. Just then there was a knock at the door, room service with our drinks. I retreated to the wardrobe, dropped the towel, and donned my silver-and-blue Dallas Cowboys robe.

"They didn't have branch water," Ellen said, tapping a pitcher. "Will crystal spring water do?"

"I suppose it'll have to." Ellen hoisted what appeared to be a double Scotch and took a hefty gulp. "You look a little shook," I said, gesturing at the couch.

She kicked her shoes off and curled up on the beige corduroy couch as I sank heavily into a leather armchair opposite. We sipped our drinks wordlessly for a minute or two, letting the quietude settle over us like healing balm after the earsplitting clamor of the Forum and the subsequent incident. Ellen's face was lined with sorrow and embarrassment. She'd forgotten to brush her hair in the excitement and raked it with her fingernails. She clicked her tongue again, a sign she was still ill at ease.

"Well, now," I finally said, "how do you feel after learning your husband is still the same surly S.O.B. he was when you left him?"

She searched the brass ceiling fixture with her eyes. "I feel…um, I feel free. Yes, free is what I feel."

"Free?"

She reached into her purse for a cigarlet. I was too tired to offer her a light. "Even though Ned and I are separated and I've had a number of—relationships—during that time, I don't think I ever shed my loyalty to Ned until tonight. I kept hoping, hoping, hoping he'd come to terms with himself."

"Or you with yourself."

"Yes," she said inhaling smoke sensuously, "I suppose so. But that would have meant my submissively accepting him the way he is, the way you saw him tonight. I've tried to be tolerant, even docile. But this"—she pointed at my scraped shin—"things like this demand more, even, than docility." She tamped the Winchester out and returned to her drink. Her cheeks, which had returned to their normal color, now tinged red again as the alcohol penetrated the tiny capillaries of her fair skin. She smiled and said, "Yes, I feel free. Or freer, at least." She gazed at me directly, as if realizing instantaneously that liberation from something also liberates you to do something else. What that could be, I made undeniably clear with my return of her gaze. Beneath the fabric of her sweater, her breasts rose and fell quickly, betraying the noncommittal stolidity of her mouth.

I got up and sat down beside her. "Ned was jealous that we were having an affair," I said.

She did not shift away from me. "I know."

"My daddy had a saying: 'You might as well be hung for a sheep as for a lamb.' "

She smiled. "You mean, if you're going to get beaten up merely for looking like my lover…" She closed her eyes and let me kiss her. Her mouth was soft and pliant and had an aroma of strawberry lipstick, Scotch, and tobacco. Our lips pressed together for a long time, but I made no attempt to exploit our intimacy with a touch of hands or even a thrust of my tongue. The kiss was so warm and satisfying, I didn't for the moment feel I needed to extend it beyond what it was.

But Ellen was not of the same mind. After another moment her lips parted and her tongue, fluid and velvety, slithered into my mouth in search of my own tongue. Her hand went to the back of my neck and her long fingers caressed me avidly, sending goosepimples the length of my body. Our tongues intertwined and played an arousing game of hide and seek. I slid my hands under her sweater.

Time stopped for a minute while I lifted the sweater off her upraised arms. She wore a thin, flesh-colored bra through which poked the half-erect nubs of her nipples. This too I removed over her head, freeing breasts larger than I'd have thought from looking at her modestly attired figure. They were exquisitely sensitive, too. The merest graze of my fingertips made her shudder and arch her back hungrily. She began panting hard, emitting little high-pitched sighs with each expiration of breath. Her pelvis ground involuntarily as I drew her nipples into nuggets with my fingers.

She reached through the gap in my bathrobe and jolted me into double-time activity with her knowing hands, cool and experienced. I reciprocated by stretching a hand under her skirt. She dosed her eyes and parted her thighs. They were smooth as marble, and she slid down to offer me the silk-clad juncture of her legs. My touch made her groan and claw my back. I pulled the elastic rim of her panty crotch and found her moistly ready. We stopped to fling off the rest of our clothes, then she slid underneath me, her well-muscled white arms beckoning to me. I buried my face in the perfumed softness of her black hair and sent shudders through her with tongue and teeth on her neck. Then I fitted myself between her legs and thrust into her. She was like warm, wet sealskin inside, and my first sweep forward penetrated to the very walls of her. She made a hissing, stuttering kind of noise akin to the pleasure-pain whimper of someone relieved of a heavy burden. I looked into her face to make sure I wasn't hurting her. I wasn't. Her pain was as sweet as my own. She urged me on with her eyes.

My hips undulated faster, and she matched me stroke for velvet stroke until our grinds blended into a blur of motion and friction that culminated with a flash-fire of ecstasy. She quivered, moaned, gasped. Then her insides convulsed around me like some huge sleek fist, yanking an orgasm out of me that I'd hoped to hold back for a much longer time.

We leveled out and returned to the tender, close-mouthed kiss with which it had all begun. Then I opened my eyes.

"Oh, Jesus," I groaned, looking at the upholstery behind her shoulder.

"What's the matter?"

"You set off another nosebleed, I'm afraid."

CHAPTER III

· · · ·

I'm not big on sleep but that night I slept till mid-morning while my body repaired the breaches rent in last night's skirmish with Ned Boudreau. My head throbbed as consciousness returned and I felt distinct stabs of pain in my shoulder, shin, and skull. I knew these would fade after a shower, a cup of coffee, and normal activity. I stretched, then remembered where I was and whom I'd spent the night with. I reached across the bed for Ellen. My fingers clutched only the flat expanse of bed linen.

"I'm over here," she said. I rolled over and peered through the open door separating bedroom and sitting room. Ellen, fully dressed and bathed in an aura of reserve as impenetrable as when we'd first met, sat in the leather armchair. The remnants of a café complet were scattered over the table beside it, and half a dozen newspapers lay in deshabille at her feet. "Shall I order you breakfast?" she asked over the top of yet another newspaper. She turned the pages rapidly, not reading so much as scanning the headlines for a particular story.

"No, it generally takes me a while to work up a hunger." I looked at her significantly. "Would you care to come in here and help me do that?"

She dropped the newspaper on the floor but didn't look at me. "I don't think so."

I pursed my lips and reflected. It's hard to place a value on any woman's turndown, even if you've just spent the night in complete abandon. With Ellen, whom I did not know well and who had a way of discouraging social intimacy even in the throes of physical intimacy—well, it could be anything from an imminent business appointment to monthly cramps to an attack of puritanical guilt. I learned a long time ago that women are as predictable as earthquakes and considerably more destructive. I did the only thing a sane man could do, I shrugged.

I reached for my robe, climbed out of bed, and closeted myself in the bathroom. A glance in the mirror confirmed what the throb in my temple and eyeballs had told me. It looked like I'd ridden a wrecker's ball into a granite wall. The agony of having to look at that bruise on my cheek and the livid yellow rings under my eyes, soon to turn dark purple, while I was shaving was more than any man should be asked to endure first thing in the morning. As soon as I got out of the bathroom, the first article of clothing I donned was my sunglasses.

As I stepped into my trousers I looked again at Ellen. She was poring over yet another newspaper, opening it full, glancing across its length and breadth like a finalist in a speed-reading contest, and flipping the page. I started to make a wisecrack, then remembered. "That's right! The newspapers!" I rushed to the pile at her feet and scanned the front page.

"It's all right," she said. "There's nothing in them about last night."

"Are you sure? There were half a dozen reporters standing there when your husband opened fire."

"I know. Their stories were all killed. I arranged it."

"You arranged it?"

"Yes. I couldn't permit that brawl to be publicized. So while you were showering last night, I called Vince Sturdevant and a few of my own newspaper connections. A little leverage applied in high places and—voilà!" She dropped the last newspaper on the carpet. "It's as if it didn't happen."

"It's recorded for posterity right here in living color, if anyone cares to look," I said, lifting my sunglasses. I hoped for an expression of sympathy.

She gave me no comfort. "That will fade soon enough."

I sat down on the couch and looked at her. "And what about us, last night? Have you managed to eradicate the evidence of that, too?"

She stiffened. "As a matter of fact, I think it best that we try."

I stiffened myself, trying not to show my disappointment. "I imagine you have your reasons?"

"Yes and it's only fair to tell you what they are. I realized this morning that my behavior last night was—was influenced by my emotional state after seeing Ned again. I was tremendously wrought up and needed a release and, well, you were there. I've been thinking about Ned and while I can't condone what he did to you, it did show—"

"That he still loves you? Thanks a lot!" Anger belched up through the depths of my head like a geyser.

"No, no, I didn't use you that way. At least, I didn't think I was using you."

"Only later, you realized how useful I'd been in helping you discover your husband hasn't lost his feeling for you." I paced around the carpet, looking for something to kick.

"If you put it that way, I suppose you're right. What we, you and I, did"—she gestured primly at the couch—"was, um, symbolic, one might say. It had nothing to do with the reality of what we are to one another."

"Which is what?"

"Strangers, Dave."

"Thanks for calling me by my first name, at least." She recognized the depth of my hurt and reached out to touch my wrist. I allowed her to and the anger drained out of me like poison from a punctured wound. "Seduced and abandoned," I sighed histrionically, "the story of my life."

She smiled. "You look like you'll survive."

"Yes," I said, gripped with sudden coffee hunger and opening the lid of the silver pot on the table. "But any time you feel like using me again—'symbolically, one might say'—you just tug my cord, okay?" The pot was empty. I went to the phone and ordered a breakfast service, on the double. When I turned around, Ellen had risen from her chair and was standing beside me.

"You're a good guy, Dave." She gave me a bland kiss on the cheek.

"Shee-it," I grunted. "If there's one thing I hate, it's being friends with a woman."

"We're also partners or have you forgotten what we're here for?" She went to the writing desk and returned with a sheet of hotel stationery with a hand-printed list on it. "While you were asleep, I went over the book and drew up a schedule of people to see. It combines the players most strongly under suspicion with the convenience of traveling plans. After another meeting late this morning with Vince Sturdevant at his office, you'll proceed to Toronto, Detroit, Bloomington, St. Louis—I've checked the NHL game schedules and it all works out. From St. Louis I thought you'd go on to Denver for a talk with Babette Laclede."

"Guy's widow."

Ellen smiled mysteriously. "Widow, yes."

"What does that mean?"

"I was thinking of The Merry Widow."

"She was glad Guy died?"

"No, it's simply that she's not the kind to mourn for very long. She has a great many…um…consolations. She had them while Guy was still alive, for that matter."

"Catty, catty," I admonished her.

"Catty, yes." Her eyes darkened and she said, "If anyone has a right to be catty…" But she never finished the sentence. "But you'll meet Babette and judge for yourself. In any event, you may be able to prod her memory about the script, where it is or who might have taken it."

"But didn't Buzzy Chambers say he visited her and she knew nothing about it?"

"Yes, but Babette's word…" Ellen swallowed that sentence, too, and it was obvious there was no love lost between her and Guy's widow. "She might very well open herself up to you," Ellen substituted. "You have a knack for doing that to a woman, I've observed."

"I seem to have lost it between last night and this morning."

She looked at me unemotionally. All trace of last night was wiped off her face like the page of a calendar torn out and thrown away. "You'll find it again."

"Where do you go from here?"

"Back to New York," she said. "There's not much more I can do until you've seen some of these people but don't hesitate to call me if there's any way I can help you. I've written my office and home numbers at the bottom of your list."

A discreet knock on the door signaled the arrival of my breakfast. Another porter was standing behind the waiter, bearing my freshly dry-cleaned blazer and laundered shirt. I dressed, packed, and ate double-time in order to hold to the tight schedule Ellen had arranged for me. The meeting with Vince Sturdevant lasted about an hour and was pretty much a rubber stamp of the strategy we'd discussed yesterday, and the schedule of interviews fined up by Ellen. Vince detailed my per diem expenses, my fee, and the bonus I could expect if I worked everything out to his satisfaction. Though his terms were generous, I put no weight of expectation on the bonus; I'd be content if I came out of this without making an ass of myself and bringing ignominy down on the National Hockey League.

Half an hour after shaking Vince's hand goodbye, I was on an Air Canada 727 to Toronto.

The flight was so short it seemed hardly worth putting the plane into the sky to get there. I had just enough time to review the portions of Guy Laclede's manuscript referring to Chub Zaretski and Ed Boniface, the Maple Leaf defenseman and wing respectively, whom Ellen had booked me to see early this afternoon.

According to Laclede, Zaretski, whose weaknesses were drinking and brawling, had mauled a customer in a Boston bar so badly the man's windpipe had closed up and he had to be rushed to a hospital for an emergency tracheotomy. The man had almost died and the operation had left him with a permanent rasp, which caused him to lose his job, selling farm machinery, on which his voice depended. The Maple Leafs paid him off and kept the matter out of the papers but the scuttlebutt had made its way around the league. Guy knew about it, and the incident was in his book.

Ed Boniface's weakness, on the other hand, was pretty girls, which is no great crime unless you're married and the father of three, and even that's no great crime if you conduct your affairs discreetly. Unfortunately, discretion does not aptly characterize the Marie Talmadge incident. Marie, a Toronto cupcake who shed the blood of virginity for the privilege of a few nights spent with the star whose pictures wallpapered her bedroom, had turned up pregnant. A good Catholic and starry-eyed with pride to be the bearer of her hero's child, she spurned the solution of abortion. So Ed Boniface had a bastard daughter. And as Guy Laclede had shrewdly pointed out in his script, the check she received every month from the Bank of Toronto was too large for mere child support, the rest, no doubt, reflected a secret agreement to keep the matter quiet.

Now, such situations, while unfortunate, are by no means unique in the world of hockey or any other professional sport. What made these different is that a man had been planning to expose them in a book and that that man had been killed.

As I'd protested to Vince Sturdevant and as I've since protested to other men who've asked me to investigate dirty business in the sports world, I'm no detective. The only long suit I bring to the detective game is common sense—common sense and sound judgment of character. If I'm capable of detecting anything, it's truths and lies. It was on this tissue-thin fabric that the "case" I built would have to rest.

I approached Zaretski and Boniface and the other players to follow them with a healthy grain of skepticism. Most hockey players are capable of murderous rages on the ice and sometimes off it. Unlike, say, baseball players, these men work in a context of contact, contact often brutal and cruel. But I do not believe they are capable of cool, premeditated murder, not even to keep a skeleton-filled closet from being opened and ruining their careers.

But I will say that of the players named in the list Ellen had drawn up for me, Zaretski and Boniface were among the most interesting. The reason is that Toronto had been in Denver for a game on the date of Guy Laclede's death.

I took a taxi directly from the airport to Maple Leaf Gardens, that venerable arena whose boards still reverberated with the memories of Syl Apps, Red Kelly, Babe Dye, Ace Bailey, Charley Conacher, Babe Pratt, and Ten Kennedy. Thanks to the letter of introduction Vince Sturdevant had given me, I was passed into the sacred precinct of the rink where the Maple Leafs were swirling in graceful practice patterns and found Ben Rymer. Ben, a slight and nervous mant who reminded me of a shrew, had taken over the coaching spot after the retirement of the legendary Red Kelly. When he saw me coming down the stairs toward the bench he leaped up to guard his territory like a miniature Cerberus. I showed him Vince's letter and he examined it with a glower.

"What's this all about, Bolt?"

"I'm afraid it's confidential," I said apologetically.

"Does Alan Eagleson know about this?" Eagleson was hockey's most formidable players' rep and head of its Players' Association. His offices were here in Toronto. For many good reasons having to do both with my official mission and my private capacity as a competitor of his, I had no desire to cross him; at the very least he could complicate things and at worst he could unwittingly wreck them by drawing the wrong inferences from the questions I was asking. Sturdevant and I had discussed this possibility this morning.

"No," I said to Rymer, "and Mr. Sturdevant has asked me to tell you not to contact Eagleson about this."

"Is there some kind of trouble?" He bit his lip and looked very grave.

"Now I know why they call you Mama Bear," I said, laughing.

He looked at me humorlessly. "If they're in trouble I want to know, that's all. And I want to help."

"I just want to ask them some questions—about someone else."

"I don't understand."

"That's all I'm permitted to tell you."

He didn't seem relieved and he turned to his bench with a headshake of apprehension. "Chub? You want to come up here a minute?" He turned back to me and said, "Ed Boniface is on the ice. Do you want me to get him, too?"

"That's okay. I'd rather see them one at a time."

Chub Zaretski, a balding blond sewer-cover of a man, clumped off the bench and up the stairs, fixing me with a scowl that I believe had been stamped permanently on his face the day he was born. "This is Dave Bolt, the players' agent," Rymer said. "He wants to talk to you, I don't know what about." Consumed with curiosity, the coach stood there until I stared him back to the bench. He looked back one more time and shouted to Zaretski, "Give a holler if you need me."

Zaretski looked at me with hollow, angry eyes. "What did that mean?"

"Oh, Ben doesn't know what this is all about and he's just being protective," I said.

"Yeah, well what is it all about, mister?"

There was no point in tippytoeing around and even some advantage in coming on strong to shock him into blurting out a revelation. "It's about Arthur Scheib, the man you punched out in Boston."

Zaretski's blond eyebrows collided to form an angry V. "How do you know about Arthur Scheib?"

"I'll tell you in a second."

"That whole thing has been taken care of. It's all on legal paper. I'll show you a copy. Scheib signed it. It says he can't hold me up for more money. It also says he won't reveal what happened to the press or anybody…"

"That's not what I'm here for."

He studied me intensely, eyebrows still beetling menacingly. Then his eyelids descended and he squinted at me with suspicion. He wagged his hockey stick slightly, but more than enough to convey a message of threatened harm. "If this is blackmail, you'd better get your tail out of here fucking-A fast, buster, or you'll spend the rest of your life pulling this stick out of it."

"Do you always talk to your blackmailers that way?" I said, watching his face carefully.

He gave me an oafish stare. "Huh? What's that supposed to mean?"

"Has anyone tried to blackmail you, Chub?"

"Not till now."

"How well did you know Guy Laclede?"

Chub Zaretski was a pretty elemental man with a face as transparent as window-glass. What was on his mind was also in his eyes and all I found in his eyes was confusion and the brute hostility of a provoked dumb animal. "Guy Laclede? I bumped into him a few times, you might say," he replied, flashing a toothless grin in a clumsy attempt at humor. "Good goalie. Too bad about him dying. He was a ballsy hockey player."

"Are you aware he knew about the Arthur Scheib incident?"

"If you say so. But he didn't know it from me, that's for damn sure. I've tried to keep it quiet but you know how guys talk. I guess it's gotten around. As a matter of fact, I been wondering what I'd do if somebody came along and tried to blackmail me. Now I know."

"Would you kill him?"

"Naw. I might make hamburger out of him but what

the hell—if it's gonna get out, it's gonna get out. I can't go around killing everybody who knows."

"You were in Denver the day Laclede died," I said. "Do you remember where you were at the time?"

His jaw squared and he leaned close to me, throwing a chilly black shadow across my vision. "Listen, Bolt, I don't know what you're fishing for but I think I'd better get my lawyer in on this."

It was a good righteous answer and, with a gut feeling that he was leveling with me, I was tempted to end the interview right there. But, at the risk of sending him into a hot rage, I decided to press just a little harder. I had a lot of people lined up to speak to and I wanted to rehearse the interrogation procedure thoroughly now. I certainly didn't want to realize, in Detroit or St. Louis or wherever my next date was, that I'd forgotten to ask a leading question back in Toronto.

I softened my voice and came on with a confidential air. "Look, Chub, I'm here on a personal errand for Vince Sturdevant." I flashed Sturdevant's letter at him. "Mr. Sturdevant has reason to believe that Laclede's accident may not have been an accident. They want me to ask around, kind of informally. If you can give me some cooperation, we can keep a lid on the matter. Otherwise, the inquiry could become formal and then all the lawyers in the world won't keep it private. Personally, I believe you're in the clear."

"In the clear? I don't even know what the fuck it's all about!"

"Just tell me where you were around the time Laclede died, if you can remember."

He searched the rafters of the building with his eyes, invoking his memory. "We were at the university rink practicing in the morning. Then the Rockies were supposed to have the rink for the afternoon. I think…um…yeah, that's right. We'd just come off the ice when somebody,

I don't remember who, came in saying they'd found Laclede's car at the bottom of a ravine or something and he
was dead. But I think it was determined later on that the
accident had occurred the night before—they only found
him the next morning, in other words."

"That's correct."

"Okay. Well, the night before—I mean, the night Laclede died—we pulled into Denver from Los Angeles. I
was bushed and just sacked in."

"Was there a bed check?"

"Sure. Mama Bear is very big on bed checks."

"Does he keep records on them?"

"No, but he'd remember if I wasn't in bed that night.
See, because of the Arthur Scheib thing, I've been kind of
on probation. Ever since then, the coach personally says
nighty-night to me every night. The guys kid me about it.
I haven't been out of line once since Scheib, believe me."

"I do believe you."

"You can ask the coach."

"No, I believe you. And do me a favor, don't tell him
what we talked about—don't tell him or anybody else."

"You can bet your ass I won't. That's all I need, is to get
mixed up in a murder rap. But I still don't understand—"

I put my hand on his shoulder. "When it's all over, I'll
explain. You want to ask Ed Boniface to come up here?"

"Ed? What did he...? Oh yeah, same thing—blackmail
again. That slut he knocked up, right?"

"That's the gist."

Zaretski smiled. "Ed couldn't kill anybody. Hell, he
can't even forecheck. He hates contact."

He returned to his bench and clambered over the barrier
onto the ice and a moment later Ed Boniface skated off and
trudged up the stairs to where I was standing. He was a

handsome kid with a mane of reddish hair and cocky green eyes, a lady-killer certainly, but not, to all appearances, a mankiller. When I introduced myself and told him what I was looking for, he started trembling and looked like he was going to cry. It took him a minute to regain his composure. "God," he half-sobbed, "it's like a nightmare. I don't know where it's going to end. You ball a chick two or three times and pay for it till the day you die. I was just beginning to think my life was stabilizing again. Now, it's shakier than ever. Murder, for Christ's sake!"

"No one's saying you're involved in murder, son," I said, starting to feel unclean, like an unsavory gossip columnist. "It's simply that Guy Laclede had the goods on a number of guys around the league and there's a possibility he was killed to shut him up. You were one of the guys he had the goods on, that's all."

"I didn't know Laclede from Adam, except on the ice."

If Ed Boniface was lying, he was very convincing. His eyes darted around the arena like a frightened doe's.

"Guy Laclede," I said, "was writing an exposé of hockey. Your Marie Talmadge affair was mentioned in it."

Boniface's complexion turned purple. "That fucking bastard!"

"Don't worry, it's not going to be published. Tell me, have you ever heard anything about a gambling scandal?"

"Oh, Jesus," he whimpered, becoming a pathetic, panicked little boy, "now it's gambling."

"Laclede hinted he was planning to expose a gambling scandal but nobody has a clue as to what it might have been."

"Don't look at me. I mean, I know of a few players who bet with each other but that's nickel and dime, you understand. I do it myself sometimes. Like when we're watching a game on TV. But never on our own games, not even to win. And never with outsiders. Shit, I don't even know any outsiders. By which I mean professional gamblers and people like that. If they hang around the Leafs, I've never seen one."

"One more thing: do you remember where you were in Denver on the night Guy was killed?"

He had just begun to relax, but now the muscles in his jaw tautened again. "It depends. What hour was he killed, exactly?"

"A little after eleven."

"Then I was in bed."

"Who with?" It was just a joke, the kind of thing I might say to any young stud but I'd forgotten that for this one it had a stinging irony and I could have bitten my tongue for making it seem as if I was taunting him.

He looked at me sullenly. "Alone, thank you."

"Can you prove that if you have to?"

"Yes. My roommate, the coach—"

"Thanks, kid. I'm sure you don't have anything to worry about."

"Will you let me know how it turns out?"

"Sure. Meanwhile, keep this between you and me, huh?"

"Do you think I'm crazy? Of course I will!"

I returned to the airport and hung around an hour until I could make my connection to Detroit. I went to the bar and had a bourbon, considerably diluted, and reflected on the day's bag. So far, pretty skimpy, but I'd sharpened up my third-degree routine and at least I'd eliminated two suspects. By "eliminated" I mean tentatively, though I didn't think either of them had lied to me, I could always come back to check out their stories if the other interviews I had scheduled proved fruitless.

The flight to Detroit was a milk hop and when I arrived I went straight to the terminal telephones to try to track down Joey Forbes, the Red Wing defenseman cited by Guy Laclede for drug use and, worse, dealing. Joey was a bachelor but a call to his pad—Ellen had provided me with his unlisted number—got no answer. I dialed some of his teammates and finally elicited that Joey often dined at Trader Vic's with a couple of other bachelor cronies and their broads. I taxied directly there and found him sitting at a boisterous corner table with two other Red Wing players, Whitey Leduc and Parker Dresden, and some very pretty girls. Joey's was a streak-haired blond teenager so young she looked five years on the wrong side of jailbait. I introduced myself and they asked me to join them.

I didn't want to make a big production of my mission and besides I was hungry, so I wrapped myself around a plate of spareribs and a Mai Tai, traded quips with the men and flattery with the girls, and only as we were rising from the table did I tell Joey I wanted to have a word with him in private. We went to the bar and talked quietly over Cognacs. The exchange was brief but, as far as I was concerned, conclusive.

Joey was a lanky, doe-eyed kid with a droopy walrus mustache and long black hair that he tied, much to the consternation of the Red Wings front office and the delight of the fans at Olympia Stadium, in a ponytail. He had inherited the bad-boy image of Derek Sanderson, except that Joey's mischief was a good deal less tolerable than Sanderson's hijinks. Brash, outspoken, and hip, Joey had boasted about his drug use the way Sanderson had boasted about his bedroom proficiency. In fact, he'd received an official reprimand, tantamount to a notice of probation, for a remark attributed to him that was published in a Time magazine interview. "I play well on ice," he had said, "but I play better on grass." He had not denied having said it when called before an NHL committee investigating drug use in hockey.

But it wasn't what he used that got him into serious trouble, it was what he dealt. He'd been arrested for selling a gross amount of amyl nitrate poppers—amyl nitrate being for speed what exploding bullets are for munitions—to a buyer who turned out to be a representative of the FBI. The affair had been covered up at considerable inconvenience to the league, who had put Joey on notice that a recurrence would mean not just banishment from hockey, but a jail term.

I told him that this incident appeared in the book Guy Laclede had been writing and waited for a shocked, frightened, or outraged reaction such as I'd gotten from Chub Zaretski and Ed Boniface. But I got no such response. Joey simply looked at me blankly and said, "Yeah? So?"

"So, if that item came to light in a book you'd be up Shit Creek without a paddle," I said, feeling faintly idiotic to have to point out the obvious.

"Fuck it," he said, cutting the air with his hand. "Everyone knows about it. It had to leak out sooner or later. What're ya gonna do—if it happens, it happens. I can't waste my time worrying about it. There's a line in the Bhagavad-Gita…"

"Did you know Laclede personally?" I said, uninterested in how the Indian scriptures justified drug-dealing.

He pulled at his ear quizzically, then sniffed. "You know something? I don't think I ever saw that dude with his mask off."

"You know anything about gambling?"

"Hockey gambling, you mean?"

"Yeah."

"Well, gambling isn't my bag, you dig, but I've heard a few things."

"Like what?"

"Like what are you looking for?"

"A major scandal."

"You mean, a fix or something?"

"Yes."

He shook his head without hesitation. "No, nothing like that. Oh, every once in a while, one of us is approached by some jive dude looking for an edge. You know, they hear half the team has the flu, they want to know if it's true. Or they sound you out to see if you're, y'know, open to suggestions."

"You mean, if you can be bribed."

"Right. But I've never seen any of our guys give them the time of day. We just walk away. I mean, none of us are angels, you understand, but when it comes to hockey, we play to win."

"Who are these people who approach you? Do you know their names? Could you identify them?"

"Not really. Just guys you meet at a bar. Or they sit down next to you at a restaurant, the way you did. They buy you a drink and get you to talk. After a few minutes you can tell they're fishing for information. But who they are, I haven't got one clue . Where you staying in Detroit?"

"I haven't booked a room yet."

"Feel free to crash with me. I'll share Bitsy with you. She gives great head."

"Thanks but I'll fend for myself. Besides, Bitsy reminds me of my daughter."

"Yeah? I'd like to meet your daughter."

"As soon as she's of consenting age, I'll be glad to introduce her to you. That's about ten years from now."

I put in at a Holiday Inn not far from the airport, watched some Johnny Carson, and hit the sack. Next morning I flew out to Bloomington, Minnesota, for a talk with Teddy Lancaster, the North Stars' coach. The subject was the story in Guy Laclede's book that Lancaster had, apparently with success, attempted to fix up Wayne Brinker, the Atlanta Flames star, with a hooker the night before a game, in the hope that Brinker would be so wasted the following day, he wouldn't play well. Brinker fell for the trick and balled the chick until the wee small hours. That Sunday afternoon, he was so lackadaisical he had to be pointed toward the enemy goal.

But what vaulted this dirty trick into an act of deplorable viciousness was that Lancaster had sent his best headhunter, Bob Fleury, out on the ice to get the nearly defenseless Brinker. Fleury threw an elbow that broke Brinker's jaw and put him out of action for a month, blowing the Flames' playoff hopes for the season.

When I confronted Lancaster, a flash-tempered bulldog, with this story, he fulminated, denying everything, threatening to sue for libel and invasion of privacy and defamation of character, and displaying such towering indignation that I found myself apologizing and retreated with my tail between my legs back to the airport. Not that I didn't think that everything Laclede had written wasn't absolutely true, it's just that I was convinced Lancaster was no more capable of killing Guy Laclede than I was.

That brought me to St. Louis that afternoon and it was a rather dejected amateur gumshoe who stepped off the plane. It was depressing enough to have drawn blanks but the prospect of drawing more of them from my still-lengthy list of suspects had begun to undermine my confidence. Was I asking the right questions? Was I getting the right answers? Was I overlooking leads? Were my instincts providing me with accurate input? Should I be checking out stories more thoroughly?

When you stop trusting yourself, you're in trouble. Your process of discrimination becomes muddy and you can't appreciate the truth when it slugs you on the jaw. I began seriously contemplating throwing in the towel.

An hour later, all that would be forgotten.

CHAPTER IV

· · · ·

St. Louis is an interesting city. Its industry is Northern, its culture Southern, and its sports tradition purely Mid-western. The typical St. Louis sports buff is incapable of dissociating poor performance from disrespect for the American flag. In the first wave of expansion following the opening up of the National Hockey League in 1967, the St. Louis Blues attracted a rabid following of which the likes were not again to be seen until the Philadelphia Flyers—the "Broad Street Bullies"—started throwing their muscle around six or seven years later.

St. Louis is also a magnet for some of your less wholesome types. But I had no idea, as I cruised west on Highway 40 in the direction of the St. Louis Arena, that by the end of the day I'd be tangling with one of them.

The arena is a buff-colored structure of Art Deco design that always reminded me of an aircraft hangar. It was a little after one in the afternoon when I unfolded out of the driver's seat of the Chevy Nova I'd rented at the airport and walked into the players' entrance looking for Jean-Philippe Boileau. The Blues had just ended practice but Boileau was still out on the ice, working on some detail too fine for me to pick up as I watched him make pass after pass at the goalie who'd agreed to stay out there to shag pucks for him. At length, satisfied I suppose, Boileau skated off and lumbered down an alley toward the locker room. I intercepted him, introduced myself, and asked him to come out with me for a drink. He shifted uneasily on his ankles, asked me a few questions that I answered with tantalizing vagueness, and finally asked me to wait outside the locker room for a couple of minutes.

I'd met Boileau once at an award dinner and though my conversation with him had been superficial—he didn't even remember me on this second meeting—he had left me with an impression of enormous sincerity and integrity. So I'd been quite dismayed, almost stupefied, to find his name in Guy Laclede's chronicle and attached to a misdeed which comes very close to the top of the no-no list, gambling. Because we cherish a certain image of athletes, a distorted one hung over from the days when they had nicknames like Bronco and Rube and Babe and Tiny, we look benignly on the player who drinks or brawls or gets girls into trouble. Indeed, we come to expect it of our athletes, it's an essential part of their "color." If players didn't make spectacles of themselves and screw up their private lives, our lust for vicarious heroes would go unsatisfied.

But we draw the line at gambling and deservedly so. For the player who gambles is not merely tampering with our image of him as a lovable, mischievous dolt, he threatens us with the alarming possibility that we have invested all this vicarious excitement in a sham. It isn't merely that gambling is dishonest that makes league and front office officials so intolerant of this sin—there are many other forms of dishonesty at which they wink. No, it's that gambling is the one transgression that loses customers and that makes it unforgivable. Guy Laclede had been absolutely right in saying that a gambling scandal could blow hockey off the ice. Everything else in his book was, when you considered it, entertainment. But gambling was nasty business and a thing of loathing to the men who ran the game.

Still, of all the kinds of gambling a player can get into, Jean-Philippe Boileau's was, if it may be said, the most honest. He placed bets with players on opposite teams and always bet his own team to win. What singled him out for special mention in Laclede's book was that Boileau bet very heavily—as much as a thousand dollars a game. You do that kind of thing often enough, you start attracting outsiders, and before long—and this is the sound theory behind rigid injunctions against player gambling, no matter what the sport—a representative of the underworld has his arm on you.

Guy Laclede hadn't said it in so many words but it was evident that if anyone had been courted by professional gamblers, it was Boileau. You wouldn't think so to look at him, though. As he stepped out of the locker room, hair damp from his shower, face glistening after a shave, shoes gleaming, slacks pressed to a knife-edged crease, he was the very model of a sports hero. He grinned confidently and told me to follow his car out to Joe and Charlie's, a popular lounge on Clayton Road where athletes and their community of supporters liked to hang out. I knew the place, having been there a couple of years before, and remembered it because the owner, Charlie Becker, stocked his bar with genuine Texas branch water, a rare treat indeed this far north.

Joe and Charlie's was scantily populated at mid-afternoon but Boileau wanted a corner table away from the other customers. He ordered a boilermaker, I a glass of twelve-year-old Tennessee bourbon and some of that ol' branch water.

While waiting I looked closer at Boileau. He was a strapping, nice-looking lad with straight black hair that receded slightly from his high forehead. His face bore a faint tracery of scars, including an inch-long scab under his left eye from a recent injury. His nose was surprisingly straight for a hockey player with six years of NHL experience behind him and his hazel eyes gazed at me with a friendly openness that proclaimed they hid nothing.

After a brief prologue and a couple of probes, I told him about Guy Laclede's book and the reference in it to him. He made a face, not so much of surprise as of disappointment. It was as if he was saying, "I knew it would come out sooner or later but I'd been hoping later."

But he said nothing. He merely looked down at the Mutt-and-Jeff figures of whiskey and beer glasses and pushed them around like players on ice. "Why do you do it, Jean?" I finally asked.

"It make me play better." His accent was thickly French and nasal.

"By raising the stake you have to lose, you mean?"

"Yes, that's a good way of putting it. If we lose a game, I don't lose just the glory. I lose the money, too. That make me real upset." He checked the beer glass with the whiskey glass. "Some guys smoke a joint or pop greenies or have a drink before a game. They say it make them play better. Me, I place a bet. But always on us to win."

"Who do you bet with?"

"Didn't Laclede say who in his book?"

"No."

"Then I prefer not to say. Just players on the other teams, that's all."

"You're sure that's all."

For the first time, his expression narrowed. "What that mean?"

"I mean outsiders."

"Gamblers? Never! I swear by all the saints, never." His fingers involuntarily flew to the golden cross dangling from a chain around his neck. He handled it nervously, looking around to see if anyone was close enough to overhear us. Isolated though we were, I got up and put a quarter in the jukebox to drown out our dialogue. "You got to believe that, Mr. Bolt," he said. He was breathing hard and his face was red.

"Have you ever been approached by professional gamblers?"

He lowered his eyes, chugged down his drink, and ordered another. He promptly downed half of that. "I couldn't say for sure whether they were professional gamblers. But there have been these…uh…guys."

"These guys?"

"Yeah, you know the kind."

"The kind that look like underworld figures?"

"I don't know what underworld figures are supposed to look like, Mr. Bolt. These aren't from out of gangster movies, you understand. But they talk like…"

"Like what?"

He scratched his chin. "Like they want something from me."

"Do you know their names?"

"One or two, yeah."

"Would you like to give them to me?"

"If you swear not to tell them you got them from me."

"No sweat."

He looked furtively around again. Stevie Wonder was doing "Superstition" on the jukebox. It would be a miracle if I heard what Boileau said to me.

"Guy named Mickey Goldblatt. Another guy named Barney Wicks."

"Anyone else?"

"Nooo…" The attenuated vowel told me he was lying.

I looked at him hard. "You're holding back on me, Jean."

His lips puckered, and a patina of perspiration formed on his forehead. "Well, this other guy I have in mind, I've never met him, you see."

"Then how…?"

"I've heard about him. In fact, I think the two I told you about work for him."

"What's his name?"

He gulped. "You sure…?"

"I gave you my word."

He muttered the name but all I heard was the soulful sigh that accompanied it.

"I didn't catch it."

"Morty Kaleeka," he repeated.

I closed my eyes. "Where have I heard that name?"

"He's big in the construction business around here. You probably seen his name on building sites. He's got a big project going up near the airport."

"Yes, that's right. But I've heard of him in some other connection."

Jean-Philippe leaned forward and put his lips practically against my ear. "Napolitani," he pronounced.

"Ah." For the first time in this weird pinball game, I'd lit up some lights. August Napolitani's was a Chicago-based mob among whose standard repertoire of nefarious activities—drugs, loansharking, prostitution, etc.—was to be found sports gambling. Which didn't mean a helluva lot, since what respectable crime syndicate doesn't indulge in sports gambling? It's a very lucrative enterprise. But it brought me closer to where I wanted to be than any other lead I'd chased down thus far and it raised some very interesting questions. "Tell me, Jean, is there a lot of gambling action on hockey that you know of? Or is Kaleeka kind of unusual?"

He shifted in his seat and wiped his brow with the back of his hand. "Look, Mr. Bolt, I don't want you to think I'm tête-à-tête with every gambler in the country."

"I don't. I'm just trying to find out how widespread gambling is in hockey. If you can help me narrow down the possibilities, you'll save me a lot of time and effort. And yourself a lot of heat, perhaps."

"Yes." He rubbed his chin for a moment. "Well, except for Kaleeka's people—these guys Goldblatt and Wicks I mentioned, I've never heard of anyone else taking hockey action. Hell, I never even knew there was a line in hockey till these characters started talking to me. See, hockey has never been much of a bargain for professional gambles. Not until now, anyway."

"Why not? And why now?"

Jean gave me a lengthy analysis which sounded remarkably like the one Guy Laclede had written—that until expansion, hockey players were dedicated Canadians whose first allegiance was to honor and glory, not money. When expansion came along with its costly price wars, players awoke to the big-money potential of their trade, and greed and envy became new factors in their mental outlook, factors which opened the door to corruption. Add to this the explosive growth of the sport in the United States, meaning a bounty crop of bettors in almost every major city, and the setup was complete.

But apparently this Morty Kaleeka was the first mobster to fully recognize this and to try to exploit it. I say "try" because Jean-Philippe Boileau couldn't think of a single instance of Kaleeka's having gotten to a player.

"Tell me, Jean," I said, "what's the likeliest way a hockey game could be thrown?"

He came back with an answer at once. "Well, there are many ways. A defenseman can let a wing break away, or maybe blow a stop in front of the goal, or maybe set himself up as a screen in front of his own goalie. He might even deflect a shot into the goal. A wing might do some of these things, too, or simply play sluggishly to hold his own team's score down. But the trouble with all that stuff is, it's not guaranteed. And if you know anything about professional gamblers, they won't touch anything that's not guaranteed. At least, that's what I've been told," he added hastily, smiling nervously. "Gamblers have to have an edge, do you see what I'm saying?"

"I do indeed. So what's the answer? The goalie?"

"Right," he said, snapping his fingers for emphasis. "A goalie, he can blow a save and look beautiful doing it, you know? Kicking his foot out, lunging for the puck, sprawling on the ice, acting disgusted, the whole bit. All he has to do is miss the puck by this much." He squeezed thumb and index finger close together until they would admit nothing fatter than a matchbook. "This much, that's all. And all he has to do it is once, twice, in a game. There's no way it can be detected."

"I see."

Jean began to warm to his subject. "Now, I'm gonna tell you something else. I don't think there's that much action during the regular season, at least not yet, not the way there is in baseball and football and basketball. That's coming, but right now there aren't enough fans who, y'know, understand the fine points."

"What are you driving at?"

"I'm driving at, it's only during playoff time that you get any real big action. That's when the whole country is watching on television. Basketball playoffs are over, baseball is too young in the season to get excited about, and except for a little tennis and golf and horse-racing, there's nothing else to watch, sportswise. So, if I was a big-time gambler, like Kaleeka, I would go after a goalie at playoff time."

"A goalie at playoff time," I repeated as if it were the inscription on a magic amulet.

"If you're looking for a gambling scandal, I would look there."

I gazed hard at Jean-Philippe. "You're sure you don't know more than you're telling me?"

His hand jumped to his cross again. "I swear to God, Mr. Bolt, may lightning strike me dead at this table."

I threw a bill on the table and pushed away. Getting to my feet, I said, "Jean, can I give you some good advice?"

Boileau was white with fear. "You don't have to say it, Mr. Bolt. After today—"

"I'll say it anyway. You better find some other way besides gambling to get up for a game. I'm bringing you this message straight from Vince Sturdevant."

He knocked a chair over getting up from the table. "Believe me, I'm cured for sure. You can bet on it." Suddenly he realized what he'd said and clapped his hand over his mouth. "What I mean by that…"

I left him in Joe and Charlie's still muttering his way out of his unintentional gaffe.

CHAPTER V

· · · ·

Morty Kaleeka's headquarters were located in a commercial-residential-shopping complex he himself had built on Franc Avenue off Clayton Road. A three-minute drive from Joe and Charlie's brought me to this conglomeration of buildings and shops done in tasteless Neo-Swiss Village. I parked in a broad lot couched in the tips of the crescent of shoe stores, boutiques, stationery stores, sporting goods stores, pizzerias and hamburger joints, and all the other retail outlets designed to support a suburban community's fantasy of the good life. I asked a checkout girl at the Woolworth's where Kaleeka's office was and she directed me to the East Wing, near the movie house.

I trudged the hundred yards to that building through throngs of glassy-eyed shoppers, a carbuncle of apprehension growing in my stomach. I'd met plenty of professional gamblers, and indeed when you have a sports operation of any kind, it's hard to avoid them. I was even on friendly terms with many, for they're a good source of information you can't get any other way. If you ever want to know what distasteful things are going on in the wonderful world of sports, you can usually buy the information for a century-note from a bookie.

But bookies are mostly punks. I'd never had the dubious pleasure of meeting anyone occupying a higher position in the underworld hierarchy. Not that Morty Kaleeka was any Godfather, at least not from Jean-Philippe Boileau's description. No, Kaleeka was just a gangland equivalent of a middle management executive, responsible to a higher power, yet not without a certain amount of juice in his own right. But if he was connected with the Napolitani organization, those same wonderful folks who gave you the Chicago Bears—Cleveland Browns scandal a few years ago, he was plugged into a pretty high-voltage circuit.

So I had good reason to be nervous. In carrying my inquiry to Kaleeka, I was in effect running my hand up forbidden skirts. That sort of thing can get a man slapped hard enough to turn his brains to mayonnaise.

Kaleeka Construction occupied both floors of a "Swiss cottage" buttressing a row of shops and a movie theater constituting the East Wing. Its reception area was furnished blandly with framed photographs of buildings the company had put up, offices and apartment houses and shopping centers of indifferent but serviceable architecture. The reception desk was manned by a big-titted, orange-bouffanted receptionist who looked at me with stupid brown eyes. She wore a tight pink sweater with silver threads running through it. When she leaned forward to ask my business, her breasts settled like underinflated tires on her switchboard. I was surprised they didn't buzz every employee in the firm and send the place into chaos.

"I'd like to see Mr. Kaleeka," I said. "My name is Bolt."

"Is he expecting you?" she said, opening a packet of peanut-butter crackers and crunching into one.

"No."

"May I tell him what this is in reference to?" Crunch nibble nibble gulp.

Oddly, I was stuck for an answer, having moved so fast I hadn't really doped out a tactic. Quite obviously, it would not do for me to tell him I was investigating a murder which he conceivably had ordered committed. Nor could I understate the case; if I didn't give him enough information, he'd think I was a Fuller Brush salesman or something and give me the bum's rush.

"Tell him I'm a friend of Mr. Napolitani," I finally said. It was a happy inspiration, though I knew I'd pay for it when he found out the truth.

The bimbo pressed a button and repeated my message. There was a muffled exchange as she described me and in none too flattering terms considering the indigo bruises still very much in evidence around my eyes where Ned Boudreau had delivered his compliments. She punched off the line and looked at me. Her eyes were still stupid but now the stupidity was mingled with suspicion, like the expression of a cow in an abattoir gazing at the man with the poleax. "Mr. Kaleeka will see you. His office is on the second floor. You may take this elevator or there's a stairs." She pointed with the remnant of a cracker sandwich at a carpeted stairway beside the elevator well.

I opted for the stairs because it might give me a better view of the layout. I paused on the first step and looked around the working area beyond the receptionist's desk. It was a typical bullpen filled with clerks and typists. To the rear stood some drafting tables on which charts and blueprints were spread before three or four young college-grad types on stools. Nobody looked more suspect of underworld associations than Debbie Reynolds might. I trod the red-carpeted stairs and, after pausing on a landing, emerged in a more flamboyant reception area presided over by a secretary who was considerably closer to my ideal, a fragile redhead with a walnut tan, limpid blue eyes, and a tongue that flicked over soft lips frequently to keep them moist. She pressed a button before I even had a chance to tell her my name and I knew she'd been alerted.

As I waited for admittance, I paced to the limits of the reception area looking beyond it for...I didn't quite know what. Like Jean-Philippe Boileau, my familiarity with underworld types was based on old George Raft and James Cagney movies plus one or two goons and gunsels I'd mixed it up with from time to time. Such people always conducted business in the back rooms of dim bars or shabby nightclubs. In the paneled luxury of these offices, I could find nothing suggesting anything but what they were—the executive precincts of a construction company. The three or four young men and women I glimpsed seemed preoccupied with nothing more illicit than conveying blueprints from one office to another or imbibing water at the cooler. One would have to conclude that whatever unlawful activities Morty Kaleeka conducted, he did not conduct them here.

But suddenly a man appeared who instantly reversed this impression. He was not a goon or a gunsel in the cliché sense but in his size and stern look, I knew he was something far from a construction engineer. The faint hint of a bulge under the lapel of his blue sharkskin jacket pegged him as a bodyguard. He had a long head with a little black thatch of hair that looked like a swatch of shag carpeting and for all I knew, that's just what it was. "YOU want to come this way, Mr. Bolt?" he said, gesturing down an aisle. His voice was baritone and sharp with the custom of commanding. His eyes did a quick rove of my body for a précis of my potential in hand-to-hand combat and the location of a gun, if any. I rounded my shoulders and put on a hangdog expression to help him underestimate me but I knew those damned black-and-blue mice flowing off the bridge of my nose and under my eyes would give the lie to my attempt to appear harmless.

He made an "after you" gesture again, forcing me to step in front of him. As I negotiated the corridor my spine quivered with a sense of his eyes boring into my shoulder blades.

I stopped before a door on which Kaleeka's name was printed in gilt. My large friend leaned against me as he reached around my waist for the doorknob. It was a subtly executed frisk, as well as a warning. His chest had the consistency of reinforced concrete and the steely lump over his heart confirmed the presence of a gun in a shoulder holster.

The door opened and I was confronted by the brilliant glare of a mid-afternoon sun pouring through a picture window and bouncing off the glass top of a desk behind which sat a bald man. I could scarcely make out his features and I quickly concluded that that was the idea. I squinted until a few details resolved themselves.

The first impression was not particularly one of menace. In fact, the sun striking his dome created a halo effect that might have been amusing to someone less apprehensive. His face was open and almost jovial, though at the moment it was clouded with curiosity and probably a little anxiety. He had small eyes and thick lips and several large purplish liver spots on his dome. He was slight of build, from what I could see, and I guessed he was not very tall.

His desk was uncluttered but beside it was a table piled high with blueprints, sketches, estimates, renderings, and scale models of buildings. As he studied me, he reached for an Erector Set model of a crane and began wheeling the miniature hook up and down. He did not rise or offer to shake hands. His bodyguard closed the door behind us and stood close to my back.

"Marie said your name was Bolt," Kaleeka opened, spinning the hook to the top of the crane.

"That's right." My eyes began to adjust. A white-on-white pattern emerged on his shirt, and a blue stripe pattern on his fashionably wide tie. His cufflinks were heavy gold nuggets with blue enamel insets.

"And you're a friend of...?"

"Mr. Napolitani."

"Who's Mr. Napolitani?" He was a good actor. His brows flowed together in a look of total bafflement.

"Just a name I was sure would get me admittance to your office," I said. "If you don't know who he is, why'd you have me sent up?"

He came back with an extemporized answer that did him credit. "I knew a guy named Bolt years ago in the service. I thought you were him. Now that I see I'm wrong, maybe you'll be good enough to leave my office."

"Don't you want to hear my business?"

"Address a letter to me," he said. "Bernie, see Mr. Bolt to the door. In fact, see him to Kansas City or Des Moines."

Bernie enclosed my bicep with a large, steely hand and tugged at it. I made no effort to resist. I moved toward the door and said, "This letter you want me to send you—is it okay if I send a carbon to the president of the National Hockey League?"

Kaleeka's eyes widened ever so slightly and he tilted his head, like a dog listening to a far-off sound. He raised a finger to Bernie and Bernie relaxed his grip on my arm. "Why would you want to do that?" Kaleeka asked. His voice was level and did not hint at anything beyond curiosity.

The next moment was crucial; if I couldn't provoke an invitation to stay and talk now, I'd be on the other side of the door in ten seconds and a golden opportunity would have been blown. I decided to drop the coy approach for something closer to a shotgun blast at close range. I shook Bernie off and looked hard at Kaleeka. "Look, Kaleeka, I got some business to transact with you and there's two ways we can do it, nice or nasty. Personally, I don't give a shit which."

He played with his crane another minute, looking unfazed. Then, without giving any impression he'd been influenced by my threat, he said, "What do you drink, Mr. Bolt?"

"I'll pass."

"Cigar?"

"Now you're talking."

"No, I'm not talking," he said with a smile, opening a brass humidor and displaying a neat rank of Upmans. "I'm only offering you a cigar."

I took one, fondled the wrapper and sniffed the heady Cuban tobacco, then nipped the tip with my teeth. "I can understand your reluctance to talk in the presence of a third party," I said, looking over my shoulder.

He clicked an ornate desk lighter and held the flame under my cigar. "Bernie? Bernie is my cherished companion and confidant." Great clouds of savory blue smoke roiled into the air, illuminated like neon by the shaft of sunlight angling through his picture window. "Now, what's all this about hockey?"

"I'm investigating hockey gambling for the NHL. I understand you might know something about it."

"Why should I?"

I sighed. "You're really going to make me dig, aren't you?"

He laughed. "I'm in the construction business, Bolt. I don't do anybody else's digging for them unless they pay me."

"Well, then," I replied, "I guess I'll just have to blast."

He shrugged. "Blast away."

"I know you're the local honcho of a gambling syndicate linked to the Napolitani crowd of Chicago. For the last few years, you've been muscling into hockey. Apparently, you've been successful enough to have done some real damage."

"Like what?"

"Like fix a playoff game." It was an educated stab, drawn from Jean-Philippe's briefing. But if it penetrated, Kaleeka didn't show it.

"A man says something like that," Kaleeka said blandly, "he really ought to have facts to support it."

It was bluff time. "I do."

"Well, then," Kaleeka answered, "don't you think I'm the last person you'd want to brag about it to? I mean, assuming everything you say about me is true, that kind of statement would surely inflame my baser passions."

"If I were worried about that, I wouldn't have come here."

He pursed his lips, confirming that I'd scored a point. "I still don't know what you know."

I thought it wouldn't hurt to say something conciliatory. "Before I tell you, let me say this, the National Hockey League is not interested in exposing a scandal to the public. On the contrary, they're determined to suppress it once they get to the bottom of it. So their interests and yours are not in conflict."

"Once they get to the bottom of it?" Kaleeka repeated, fast on the pickup. "That means they don't know anything, they just suspect it." He drew on his cigar and hissed out a long stream of smoke. His expression was one of satisfaction. It was about to change.

"They don't know anything, no," I replied, tamping ash into a marble ashtray on his desk. "But Guy Laclede did."

Bingo! His eyes widened and narrowed in quick succession and he rubbed his nose. Not what you'd call hysterical reactions, but in a cool dude like Kaleeka, they shone like beacons. A rustle behind me told me Bernie had been jolted out of his torpor by the mention of Guy Laclede's name.

Kaleeka took a deep breath and seemed to recover his composure. "Guy Laclede—wasn't he killed a few weeks ago?"

"I'm sure you'd know the answer to that question better than anybody else."

This dangerous wisecrack pricked Kaleeka visibly. His fingers nervously drummed on the cylinder of his cigar and blue veins in his temple began to throb. "Let's get something straight, Bolt. Granting that everything you said is correct—which I'm not about to do—if you're suggesting that he was killed to shut him up..."

"Isn't that a logical conclusion?"

"Maybe, but it's the wrong one. And a stupid one to imply to my face, considering that I could have your head severed from your body before the day is three seconds older. Sure, I'll admit that...that someone in the hypothetical position we're talking about would be very relieved to see Laclede dead, if Laclede knew something damaging. After all, dead men tell no tales. But—"

"But this one did."

A sheen of perspiration glistened over Kaleeka's upper lip. "What do you mean?"

"You know perfectly well what I mean. You knew Guy was writing a book in which he planned to expose what you did."

Kaleeka jumped to his feet, squealing. "What?" His little eyes bulged and his mouth hung open fatuously. He stood frozen in horror for a long ten seconds, during which I scrutinized his face for a false note. If he was faking shock, he was the best actor to come down the pike since John Barrymore.

But his shock was nothing compared to mine. I'd been positive I had my man, that the trail of investigation led to the headwaters of Kaleeka Construction Company. I'd already congratulated myself on my expert handling of this complex and delicate matter and banked the handsome fee Vince Sturdevant had promised me. But in Kaleeka's thunderstruck face was the tale of my gross miscalculation.

All kinds of alarms started clanging in my head as I realized the danger I'd precipitated. For now that Kaleeka knew there was a script, he'd want it. He'd want to know what was in it and what it said about him. And he would undoubtedly kill to find it and suppress it. These same realizations were even now flooding into Kaleeka's quick mind. I could see the lines in his face transforming from horror to outrage to guileful calculation. In another moment, he'd order Bernie to seize me and God knew where the trip would end.

Without another second's reflection, I grabbed the marble ashtray off Kaleeka's desk and rose, swinging the ashtray at Bernie's head in one twisting discus-like motion.

Bernie had not been able to interpret Kaleeka's astonishment as a prelude to action and so my charge caught him flatfooted. But he had catlike reflexes and jerked his head back just enough to make me miss my target, his temple. The ashtray struck his left cheekbone and I heard a sharp crack like a dry twig snapping. I'd probably fractured it. But that wasn't enough to knock him out of commission. As he fell back, he swiped at me with his right hand and got my shirt, pulling me down on top of him. I tucked my knees under me so as to land cannonball fashion on his solar plexus. He grunted and his own knees involuntarily sprang up, striking my spine with the impact of a medicine ball. But I managed to keep my balance astride his chest. He swung blindly with his right fist but I blocked it with my left and brought my right, ashtray still clutched in it, down on his head. This time I didn't miss, catching him square behind the ear. He twitched once and went limp.

I looked up to see what Kaleeka was doing. He had one hand on an intercom button and had just yelled something into it. His right hand was groping around his desk drawer —for what, I could too easily figure out. I darted my hand under Bernie's lapel and found a snubnosed.38, a "Banker's Special," in its shoulder holster. I whipped it out and trained it on Kaleeka's heart. "Hold it, Kaleeka," I barked.

He froze. "Watch out with that thing, Bolt."

I gestured wildly, making him flinch and cower. "Take your hand out of that drawer. Slowly."

He withdrew his hand and raised it with the other, backing away from the desk. "What the hell is this, you crazy bastard?"

I stood indecisively in front of him, trying to figure out what to do. Bernie moaned and began coming to, writhing and clutching his face. I wasn't worried about him but Kaleeka had obviously summoned help. I looked around the room for an escape route, but the only exit was the door I'd come in through and any moment that way would be blocked by Kaleeka's reinforcements.

Kaleeka sensed he was in command, and relaxed. "What about this book you say Laclede was writing?"

"I've already told you too much about it," I said, going to the windows. "I thought for sure you knew about it and had him killed and destroyed the script. Jesus, don't you build fire escapes on your buildings?"

"This is the first time I've heard of the script!" he shouted. Then he cocked his head as something occurred to him. "What do you mean, you thought I had the script destroyed? You mean you don't have it? You mean, it wasn't found, they don't know where it is?" He rubbed his temples. His face started to get purple. "You mean that fuckin' script is floating around somewhere, nobody knows where? Jesus fucking Christ!"

I made up my mind and motioned with my gun to the door. "Let's go."

He frowned. "Go where? What's this?"

"I'm borrowing you for a hostage."

"You're insane. You don't understand who you're..."

"I said let's go!" I took a menacing step toward him and he quickly sidled out from behind his desk. He was short, maybe five-six, but stockier than I'd thought, to see him sitting behind his desk. Though I had nine inches on him, I suspected he was a ferocious scrapper and I kept a goodly distance from him. He opened the door, looked at me, and smiled. I looked over his shoulder.

At the end of the corridor, four men stood brandishing guns. One was black, the others white. They wore construction workers' clothing, oil-smudged chino pants, checked flannel shirts or glossy windbreakers, and heavy boots, but dress them in purple jerseys, tights, and helmets, and they could have been Marshall, Page, Eller and Larsen, the Minnesota Viking front four. They made no attempt at concealment, but filled the corridor insouciantly, confident they had me cornered. A moment later, they started to advance.

I wrapped my left arm around Kaleeka's throat and pressed Bernie's gun against his temple. The goons stopped and watched, still confident but waiting for a signal from Kaleeka. I tightened my forearm lock around Kaleeka's neck, choking him. "Call them off," I said in his ear.

I had to hand it to him for guts. He held out long enough to worry me. I locked my grip, cutting off his windpipe. The four men at the end of the hall watched with morbid fascination as the life drained out of their twitching leader. I felt a strange elation and wondered if I'd be able to stop short of completing the act of murder. It must have been this that Kaleeka sensed. With his last energy, he waved his hands at his men and they began to back off. I loosened my grip. He gasped stertorously, then began to choke and sputter.

"Put your guns on the floor and back off," I instructed them.

They kneeled and laid their pieces down. Then they got to their feet again and retreated a couple of paces.

My wrist still clotheslined under Kaleeka's jaw, I urged him forward until we stood over the guns. Two were .38 specials, one was a long-barreled .32, and the last was a clumsy but lethal army issue .45 automatic, bluing bleached almost silver by constant cleaning. I wasn't sure just what to do with this arsenal and didn't have much time to debate about it. Then I noticed a tall cylindrical ashtray outside an office door, with a dish of white sand in it.

I let go of Kaleeka and made him step against the wall, nose touching the concrete. I shifted my gun to my left hand and held the muzzle to his coccyx while I kneeled down. I picked up the guns one at a time, scooped the sand out of the ashtray with their barrels and rubbed their actions in the pink and white grit, rendering the weapons temporarily useless.

"Now, boys, step into Kaleeka's office," I said nutcrackering Kaleeka's neck again and pressing against the wall to let the four file past me. They trudged in front of us like a troop of irritable baboons, entered Kaleeka's office, and stood in the doorway glaring at me. "I'm taking your boss for a ride. I'll let him go as soon as I'm clear. But try to follow me and I'll leave a nice trail of your boss's skull fragments to make it easy for you. How's that, clear enough?"

"Do as he says," Kaleeka gurgled through the clamp of my arm.

They closed the door, but I didn't believe they'd follow my order. I dragged Kaleeka back up the corridor and waited outside his office door. After a moment the doorknob turned and the door slowly opened. A black face peered tentatively out. What he saw was the snout of my gun sitting against his upper lip. "Wasn't it Damon Runyon who said, 'Life is three-to-two against'?" I said to him. He closed the door quickly. I figured that bought me five or ten minutes.

As I started to shove Kaleeka back down the corridor, he dug his heels in and said, "Listen, Bolt, my employees, they don't know—y'know, they don't know about me. Can't we just walk out of here without…?" He pointed at my gun with his thumb. "Besides, if they call the police…"

It didn't sound like a trick. "You promise to behave yourself?"

"Yeah, yeah," he said with a resigned sigh.

"Okay." I released him and thrust the revolver into my blazer pocket. We sauntered through the second-floor reception room, where Kaleeka told his gal we were going out for an hour or two and saluted her with a friendly wave. We trotted down the stairs to the first floor past Marie, now nibbling on a Mars Bar, and into the parking lot.

I drove the Nova out of the lot with my right hand, covering Kaleeka with the gun in my left, resting in my lap. I drove back to Clayton Road until we came to Brentwood, where I hung a right back to 40 West away from the city of St. Louis and into the rural countryside. I scanned the road looking for a nice inconvenient place to drop Kaleeka. The little man sat calmly, his former mask of cool indifference restored to his face. Finally, he looked at me. "This book Laclede was writing, have you seen it?"

"Some of it."

"What exactly does it say? Does it mention me by

name? Does it go into detail about…y'know?"

"Enough detail to make it a dangerous document to be kicking around unclaimed."

"That doesn't answer my question."

"Why should I put your mind at ease?"

"Because maybe I can help you. Like you said, the league and I are basically interested in the same thing, finding that script and suppressing its contents before it gets into the wrong hands."

"That's true, but I don't think they'd cotton much to the idea of having you as an ally—they wouldn't endorse your methods."

"At least tell me—"

"This looks like a nice place for a nature walk," I said, pulling off onto a shoulder just past a sign that announced the town limits of someplace called Crevecoeur.

He looked bleakly at the heavily forested roadside. Traffic was moderate in both directions and he'd have no trouble hitching a ride. But by that time, I'd be long gone. He opened the door and looked at me with icy gray eyes, flecked with green, like an angry sea. "Okay, Bolt. I'm not asking you anymore, I'm telling you. You'd better find that script and when you do, I'm the first person you're going to show it to. The first and the only one. For which I may permit you to live, I haven't decided yet."

"Gee, Mr. Kaleeka," I grinned. "You'd think you had the gun trained on me."

"I do, Bolt. Wherever you go from now on, you're gonna be lined up in my sights. Do you catch my meaning?"

"There's a bluebird, Mr. Kaleeka, Missouri's state bird. Why don't you trot over to that tree yonder and take a closer look at it? Report it to the Audubon Society when you get back to St. Louis."

He stepped out of the car, slammed the door, and leaned in through the window. "Remember what I said, Bolt. I want that script and I'm going to have it."

Then he pivoted and sauntered away in the direction of Missouri's state bird.

CHAPTER VI

· · · ·

As I cut across the broad grass island for a U-turn onto 40 East back to St. Louis, I noticed in my mirror that Kaleeka was studying my license plate. The man was smart. Within minutes after getting to a phone, he would be able to trace the car to the Hertz Airport Rental lot, he might already know that's where it came from if he noted the Hertz tag affixed to the license plate frame. The airport was a twenty-or thirty-minute drive; I might find more than a pretty girl waiting for me at the Hertz desk when I returned the keys.

Then I realized I wasn't the only one in jeopardy. I swung off onto the first exit I came to and drove south looking for a public phone. After half a mile I came to an Exxon station. A phone booth stood beside the air pump. A uniformed attendant who looked like he needed the business stepped out of the office, then shrugged and returned to his desk when he realized I was no customer for him today.

I went to the trunk of my car and went through some papers in my overnighter until I found the list of addresses and phone numbers Ellen had given me. Halfway down the list was Babette Laclede's, in Denver. I chucked a dime into the phone and tapped the booth window impatiently. It took a maddening minute to get the operator and give her my credit card number. The phone buzzed six times before Guy Laclede's widow picked it up.

"'Allo?" Her voice was sleepy and petulant as if she'd been napping or making love. Her greeting was rich with French-Canadian inflexion and extremely sexy.

"Mrs. Laclede?"

"Yes?"

"The name is Dave Bolt. I'm calling about the script your husband was writing."

I interpreted the ensuing silence as puzzlement and tried to picture the woman at the other end of the line, using only the monosyllables she had spoken and the bitchy remarks about her that Ellen had made. Guy Laclede had been in his early thirties, his wife would be the same age, give or take a year, a woman in the full bloom of early maturity. No, make that fading. Married to Laclede, her life would have been devoid of glamour except for the Stanley Cup play-offs several years ago in Chicago. Boredom and drudgery would have taken its toll on her youth. She would not be particularly attractive, but robust in a Gallic way, heavily made up, fun-loving and lusty, beautiful only when the prospect of capturing a man for the night forced her to make an effort. Her enemy would be bright daylight.

"Yes," she finally said, "I'm listening."

"I've been asked by Vince Sturdevant to look into certain questions concerning it."

"I have told everything to Buzzy Chambers," she sighed edgily.

"Yes, but I'd like to hear it again, straight from you. But that's not what I'm calling about."

"Oh?"

"Your husband knew something very damaging to a certain underworld figure. That man has just learned about the book and he wants it. I mean, he wants it bad, if you follow my meaning."

"But I don't have the script! I don't know where it is. I say this and say this." Her voice was querulous and weary. "Don't they believe me?"

"We can discuss that later. But listen to me carefully. Some of these gangsters may be boarding a plane for Denver very shortly and they'll be coming to your house to search for the script themselves. So please remove yourself from your house at once, go to a friend's or something. You may only have two or three hours. I'm taking the next plane out there from St. Louis and will be staying at the Mile High Motel. Leave a message for me there and I'll get together with you this evening, got that?'"

"Yes, very well."

"I know you got a lot of questions," I said, "but they'll just have to wait. Please do as I say. These people are rough."

"I understand."

I started to place the phone on its cradle but changed my mind and put it to my mouth. There was one more thing I wanted to say to her, it would not improve my public relations image with her but it really had to be said. "And Mrs. Laclede?"

"Yes?"

"If you do have that script, put it in a safe place, okay?"

I hung the phone up in the middle of a jabber of protest.

I ran back to the car and had driven it no further than the perimeter of the gas station when something dawned on me. I hit the brake and clapped my palm to my head. "Oh, Dave Bolt, you asshole!" I slammed the shift into reverse and dragged backwards at forty miles an hour to the phone booth. The proprietor of the station bolted out of his chair in the office with a horrified look and covered his eyes. I stopped a foot short of the booth and jumped out of the car, leaving door open and motor running.

I had assumed that if Kaleeka was going to send a raiding party to Denver, he would dispatch it from St. Louis. Now I realized he didn't have to. With his Napolitani family connections, all he had to do was to call some colleagues in Denver and have them drop in on Mrs. Laclede and sit on her till Kaleeka or his lieutenants arrived. Contrary to what I'd told her, she didn't have a couple of hours, she might only have a couple of minutes.

As I dug into my pants pocket for a dime, my memory flashed back to one of my first games as a Dallas Cowboy—it was against the San Francisco 49ers. Earlier that week in a practice session Coach Landry had told me, "Remember this: playing-errors are forgivable, but thinking-errors—never." Well, in the 49er game I dropped an easy square-out pass and it almost cost us the game—a playing-error if there ever was one. Yet Coach Landry yanked me out so fast it felt he'd slung a hook through my jersey. "That was unforgivable," he said.

If that was unforgivable, there was no word for the thinking-error I'd just committed. I cursed myself viciously as I went through the rigamarole again of phoning Babette Laclede.

The line was busy.

I stared at the phone as if dirty looks could clear the line. I hung up, waited thirty seconds, and tried again.

Still busy.

Two more times and still busy.

I asked myself who I knew in Denver.

I had some clients there, a basketball player with the

Rockets, who were now in Los Angeles for the first round of NBA western conference playoffs; two football players with the Broncos who were probably fishing or golfing during the off-season; and Paul Beauregard, the Denver Rockies goalie who had replaced Guy Laclede. I dialed area code 303 and the Information number, 555-1212, and got Beauregard's number. I called him, wondering if the Rockies were home today. There were only one or two games left in the NHL season.

I got Paul's wife, who chirped a greeting and summoned her husband to the phone. "Paul, it's Dave Bolt."

"Dave! Hey, pal. You line me up for a Rapid Shave commercial or something?"

No time for banter. "No, this is serious. Do you know Babette Laclede?"

He uttered a lubricious chuckle. "Who doesn't know Babette Laclede? She's the team mascot. Hell, she's the league mascot!"

"All right, listen, for reasons I can't go into, there may be a car full of goons on the way to her house this very moment. Can you quickly assemble a garrison of three or four guys and get over there pronto to hold down the fort till I arrive?"

At last, he became solemn. "Jesus, Dave, what the hell is it?"

"I can't explain now."

"What about the police?"

"I don't want the police in on it."

There was a silence. "Is this on the up-and-up?" he said at last.

"Yes," I said, getting a little frantic, "but I just don't have time to run it down for you."

I could hear him turning it over in his mind. "What if these jokers have guns?"

"Do you have a gun?" I answered.

"Boy," he said, "this is getting pretty heavy." I could picture him rubbing his neck and breaking out into a sweat.

"All you'll have to do is fire a warning shot across their bow," I said reassuringly. "I don't think they'll want to lay siege to a defended house in the suburbs."

"That's true. I have a hunting rifle, thirty-thirty."

"That's fine."

"What the hell did she do, Dave?"

"Please, Paul," I pleaded, "there's no time now. Just get over there and save that girl's ass."

"Okay, okay. And don't worry. We've all become very fond of that girl's ass."

Somewhat relieved, I got back in the car, swung north until I hit 40 East, then gunned the Nova as fast as I dared, heading for the airport. It had taken almost fifteen minutes to transact this business and I hoped that that wasn't enough time for Kaleeka to get to a phone. It took me another fifteen to get to the airport. I made my way warily to the Hertz desk, surveying the faces in the terminal for a glimpse of the ones I'd confronted at Kaleeka's office. I was in luck. So far, no reception committee.

After checking in with Hertz, I double-timed it over to the American Airlines ticket counters. I waited for a couple of honeymooners with sixty pieces of luggage to weigh in, then stepped up to a crewcut young man with a rosy face who took keen relish in having memorized not just his own airline's schedule, but the schedules of all the others as well. "Our next flight to Denver is at six forty-eight," he beamed.

I looked at my watch. It was five after six. "Nothing earlier?"

"Not on American, sir. There's Continental flight one-eight-one leaving at six-thirty, but that has intermediate stops at Kansas City and Topeka, and will actually get you into Denver half an hour later than our own non-stop—thirty-two minutes, to be precise. Also, ours is a dinner flight."

I pondered the choices. If Kaleeka was sending men to Denver, he'd put them on the fastest plane, the American flight leaving at 6:48. Obviously, I didn't want to be on the same plane as they. But I couldn't take the Continental flight knowing I'd pull into Denver a half-hour after them. I looked around the terminal but there was still no sign of Kaleeka or his Purple People Eaters. "Book me on the American flight," I said, flipping my American Express card across the counter. The transaction took six or seven minutes. I went to the phone and called Babette Laclede again. Her line was still busy. My stomach began to flutter. Could she have been on the phone with the same person all this time? Five different people? Had she taken the phone off the hook for some reason?

Or had someone taken it off for her?

It was 6:15. I decided to run down to the Continental gate to see if Kaleeka's men had decided to take the 6:30 flight. I looked at a closed-circuit television set suspended over the Continental Airlines desk. The 6:30, Flight 181, was scheduled for boarding at Gate 15.

I closed my eyes for a moment to think things through. Then I headed for the escalator to the lower level of the terminal. Stepping off near the luggage caravels, I went to a bank of lockers, dropped a quarter into locker Number 4948, and stealthily inserted the .38 I'd taken off Kaleeka's bodyguard. All airline terminals have a security checkout area, and little as I cared for the notion of parting with my weapon at this critical juncture, I cared even less for the idea of being nabbed for possession after passing through the electronic scanners and setting off the sirens.

I had no idea if I'd ever reclaim the gun, but I hooked the locker key to my keyring anyway.

I went to a trash basket and pulled out a neatly folded Post-Dispatch and carried it to the checkout area at the entrance to gates 10 through 20. I flashed my blue boarding pass at the security guard, laid my overnighter on the moving belt, stepped through the metal detector while my bag glided through the fluoroscope and collected the suitcase at the other end.

I entered the long, brachiated walkway leading to gates 10 through 20, my eyes flicking to all points of the compass for a glimpse of undesirable faces. The corridor was busy and stuffy and smelled like kerosene, the ever-present airport odor of jet exhaust. The air whined with the pre-and post-flight revs of commercial jet aircraft and the gentler thrums of prop craft that scooted in and out of the array of silver monsters, looking for takeoff clearance or a route to their hangars.

I reduced my pace as I approached Gate 15, and peered cautiously into the waiting area. It was sparsely populated. Boarding hadn't been announced yet. I saw no one who looked potentially injurious to my health.

I positioned myself opposite, inside the waiting area at Gate 16, and buried my nose in a Post-Dispatch article on wardrobes for pregnant mothers. From time to time, I'd lower the paper and pan the lounge across the corridor but no one of interest showed up.

I learned that many notable designers including Geoffrey Beene and Scaasi were designing evening gowns for mothers in advanced pregnancy and the prices could run as high as five hundred dollars.

After another minute, boarding for Continental Flight 181 was announced and the passengers filed through a door onto the ramp leading to the plane. I maintained my vigil until 6:30 when the ramp was withdrawn and the plane, a Boeing 727, taxied away. At least I knew what flight they weren't on.

I checked the television again and learned that my own flight, American 496, was scheduled for boarding at gate 19. I edged along the wall toward the end of the boarding alley. Perhaps all these precautions were groundless. Perhaps Kaleeka hadn't thought of trying to extract the script from Laclede's widow or had decided that since we'd probably visited her ourselves, he'd simply be duplicating our futile efforts. Perhaps he was indeed calling up some local Denver hoods rather than sending his own men there. And perhaps, if he was sending his own men from St. Louis, they would be on a later flight. Nevertheless, I had to be alert for the worst contingency. And it was lucky I was. Because when I peeked around the wall into the Gate 19 lounge, they were there, the ones I called Page and Larsen, standing at the desk getting seat assignments.

I did an about-face and hustled back up the walkway in the direction of the waiting room. I stopped at a phone and called Babette Laclede again. Again a busy signal. I remained in the phone booth a minute to think. I was booked on the same flight as Kaleeka's goons, a fact that created some sharp limits on my plans for a long and placid life. I realized they could not be armed unless they'd somehow managed to sneak guns past the checkout area but this was cold comfort, for no doubt they could find some other way of dispatching me. A professional killer can do more with a seat cushion or airsickness bag than most people can do with a submachine gun. Yet I could not afford to let them get to Denver ahead of me, even though I had friends guarding Babette—hell, because I had friends guarding Babette. This was my own quarrel and it was wrong to involve innocent men in it. I had to get to Denver first. But how?

I thought of chartering a private plane but that might take too much time to line up and even a small jet might not beat a Boeing 727 to Denver. Maybe I could get Kaleeka's men off the plane at the last moment using some ruse. But that was risky.

Still perplexed, I pushed open the door of the phone booth. An old man was standing there waiting to use the phone. He held his boarding pass in his right hand. It had the American Airlines symbol on it but it was red. Mine was blue.

"Excuse me, sir," I said to him. "What does a red boarding pass mean?"

He examined his pass as if he hadn't known what color it was. "Means first class, I guess. The man at the counter gave a blue one to the folks in front of me and I heard them ask for coach."

"Thank you very much," I said, shaking his hand and leaving him bewildered.

Once again I approached Gate 19, letting a group of tourists run interference for me. Concealed in a knot of babbling geriatric cases, I walked past the gate and glanced into the lounge. My friends were standing at opposite walls surveying the passengers. One was scratching his nose with his boarding pass, the other had his pass tucked into the handkerchief pocket of his sports jacket.

The passes were blue.

I looked at my watch. I had about ten minutes. I raced back up to the main waiting room and ticket counters. I stepped in front of a line of passengers waiting to see the crewcut guy who'd sold me my ticket. Shutting my ears to their grousing, I said, "Can I swap this for first class?"

"Not for free."

"That's okay," I said, slapping my credit card down.

He looked at me ruefully. "I was waiting on this lady."

"This is a life-and-death emergency," I said, apologizing to a blue-haired matron.

He'd heard that one before, I'm sure, but with her tacit assent, he wrote up the change, stuck a gummed label on my ticket, and slid the papers back across the counter. During this transaction, which took two minutes, I'd been planning the rest of my strategy.

I ran over to the row of concessions off the main waiting room and ducked into the drugstore, which also sold toys, games, and novelties. I scanned the shelves for something I might use to disguise myself with and found one of those Groucho faces with rubber nose, heavy black mustache and eyebrows, and horned-rim glasses. Outlandish, but with some adaptation it would serve.

I bought it, plus a boxful of children's paper cutouts, from which the only thing I wanted was the paste. I looked at my watch. Five minutes left.

Two doors down from the drugstore was a sportswear shop. I grabbed a peaked cap out of a bin on the counter, threw a bill at the lady, and ran out without waiting for my change. I ducked into a men's room. Four minutes left.

I tore the Groucho ensemble apart and burrowed into the cutout set until I'd torn a tube of paste from its hard-plastic container. With the hair from the Groucho mask, I built myself some semblance of a dark mustache, eyebrows and sideburns, and pasted them on. I threw the horned-rim glasses away but donned my own dark shades, then the peaked hat, which was unfortunately designed for a macro-cephalic. It rested uneasily on my ears and would undoubtedly slip over them when I walked. I reached into my trouser pocket, took my handkerchief out, crumpled it into a ball, and stuffed it into that hat, which at least prevented it from collapsing around my nose even if it made me look like a Dead End Kid. Three minutes left and there was still the problem of my distinctive camelhair blazer and brown sports shirt. I needed a coat.

In the bathroom mirror, I saw a pair of legs under the door of a stall. The guy's trousers and underpants were dropped around his ankles. Slung over the stall door was a battered raincoat. I felt a twinge of remorse for taking advantage of a man in such a pathetically vulnerable position but this was no time to indulge my conscience. I reached into my wallet and tossed a pair of twenties under the door of the stall. "Thanks, pal," I said, grabbing the coat and running out of the bathroom. Two minutes left. I donned the coat as I ran.

Had I known that the poor slob was built along the lines of Mickey Rooney, I might have sought better pickings. His coat was so tight under the arms I couldn't lower them without ripping it from stem to stern. But at least it covered my clothing.

I went through the security checkout area again with a minute left and raced to the gate just as the last passengers were boarding. There was no sign of Kaleeka's men. They had probably waited till the last second, then boarded. I was the last passenger to embark.

Rounding my shoulders, I stepped aboard. An amply built black stewardess greeted me with a plastic smile and obvious distaste in her eyes. This meant my disguise was a success. I hadn't had time to check out my total effect in a mirror but I'm sure I looked, to use one of Trish's favorite expressions, like a great big schmuck. At least I sure as hell felt like one.

I slid into my window seat on the right side of the first-class section, at the rear against the bulkhead dividing first class from coach. The two compartments were joined by a corrugated plastic partition. Sooner or later, I was certain, a representative of Kaleeka Construction Company would wander through from the coach section and look over the passengers in the first-class compartment. I decided I was at a disadvantage near the window and, as the aisle seat beside me was vacant, I shifted to it. When Page or Larsen came looking for me, he'd have to look down at a poor angle. And if he recognized me, I'd be in a better position to leap out of my seat.

It happened sooner than I expected. The cabin door had no sooner been slammed shut than the black dude, the one I called Alan Page, poked his head in and peered around the compartment. I didn't have time to get my newspaper up, which was just as well, as it might have aroused his curiosity about the man behind it. I played it cool, reaching into the pocket of the seat in front of me and removing the emergency instruction card, which I studied like an anxious first-time passenger. The man looked at me and I sucked in my breath and steeled my legs for a spring to my feet. The emergency instruction card didn't say anything about what to do when your would-be assassin recognizes you on an airplane.

But he didn't give me a second glance, and if he was inclined to, the stewardess thwarted him. "I'm sorry, sir, but you'll have to take your seat now. We're preparing for takeoff."

He grunted and left the compartment. The stew closed the partition and went into her emergency instruction routine, during which time I was emitting great gusts of relief and nervously fingering the airsickness bag in the seat pocket. For several moments, I thought I was going to need it.

What I really needed was a drink and they couldn't get this great silver bird into the sky soon enough to suit me. As soon as we reached cruising altitude and the booze wagon came around, I ordered a double bourbon and water. It wasn't branch water but taste in this instance was secondary to effect and moments after the first sip I felt my nerves disjangling for the first time in what seemed like a week. The aroma of dinner warming in the galley reminded me I hadn't eaten all day. When my tray arrived, I placed it on the drop-table of the window seat and ate off it catty-corner to keep myself free of obstructions; if Page had recognized me or wandered in for a second look, I didn't want a table full of food hindering the course of my fist towards his face. The stewardess knitted her eyebrows at this odd spectacle but as she'd already written me off as Superflake she left me to my roast turkey, lyonnaise potatoes, salad niçoise, and double bourbon.

The flight was uneventful but when the plane dipped as it picked up the descent signal from Denver, my anxieties began to rise again and I contemplated my move when we deplaned. I felt I had a good chance, as they say on the quiz shows, to beat the other couple. For one thing, I'd be first off the plane, the exit being through the first-class compartment near the cockpit. More importantly, I was fairly certain Page and Larsen would have to wait for their luggage because it contained their guns. Having checked my gun in the locker at St. Louis, I'd been able to carry my overnighter on board and stow it in the luggage rack. That meant I might have as much as a fifteen-minute jump. I was tempted to call Babette as soon as I was in the terminal but conservative thinking militated against it. It could just be that these guys had somehow managed to smuggle their guns on board, or hadn't packed them, or in the interests of speed would decide to leave their luggage in the terminal and head straight for Babette's house. Not knowing I'd provided her with an armed guard, they might figure they'd need nothing more than muscle to gain entry to her house.

I was first in line when the plane pulled up to the terminal and bolted through the exit like a sprinter coming off the blocks. I'm sure the stew was glad to see the last of me.

I dashed through the terminal, following the signs pointing to transportation to downtown Denver. I looked once over my shoulder and saw no one pursuing. I climbed into a taxi and instructed the driver, a plump, gray-haired old dude who smoked Camels incessantly, to take me to Windwood, a suburb, address 414 Jefferson Street.

The ride took fifteen minutes, which I occupied by perpetually twisting my head around to see who was following me. No one, so far as I could make out.

Windwood was a newly created suburb carved out of a hill from which the view of the blue, snow-tipped Andirons, the foothills to the Rockies, shimmered in the crystal air. The sun hovered a few degrees above the jagged peaks, igniting a few wispy mares' tails to incandescent purples and oranges. We climbed a steep and winding road and after a minute turned into Jefferson, a pleasant street lined with dogwoods and forsythia only just blooming in the late cold spring of the mile-high city and aspens whose fresh silver and green leaves fluttered like millions of tiny kites in the faint evening breeze. Altogether, the most agreeable of settings for a deadly shootout.

The Laclede house was a boxy yellow cottage set back about twenty yards from the street and surrounded by young crabapple trees. A slate path led to the side of the house where a porch framed the front door. The windows facing the street were curtained and mute and I suddenly felt a paralyzing sense of uncertainty, for I realized I wasn't sure who, if anyone, was in that house.

I was about to ask my driver to wait when I noticed, in the car parked in front of the house, a slight movement. I gazed at it and in the encroaching dimness of sunset made out the top of someone's head. I got out of the taxi and tiptoed, head down, along the curbside rear fender of the parked car, an old Chrysler sedan, and cautiously raised my head for a look into the window of the rear door.

Suddenly the door burst open, slamming my groin and knees. I stumbled backwards and saw an orange blur as a big man in a lumberjacket sprang out of the car, seizing me as I hit the turf of the front lawn. He landed full on top of me, ramming the wind out of my lungs with his knees and pinning my throat with his forearm. He was tremendously strong but I had my fists free and rained blows indiscriminately on his head, which did more harm to my knuckles than his skull. Then my arms were jerked backwards by another unseen man, I was pinned to the ground and the barrel of a hunting rifle was thrust into my cheek. "Flinch and you're a dead man, motherfucker," the bearer of this weapon growled. I relaxed and sighted up the barrel at a tall—gigantic from my worm's-eye viewpoint, lanky guy with a bush of wild reddish hair and a droopy auburn mustache.

Between the wind still rushing out of my lungs and the wrist of my assailant on my windpipe, it took several moments before I got a sound out. Finally, I managed to gurgle a message. "Paul, it's me, you silly asshole. Dave."

He gazed at me with brown eyes devoid of recognition and I realized to my horror that I'd forgotten to remove my disguise. He leaned over for a closer look and pried my cap off with the barrel of his rifle. "Oh, Jesus, Dave, that is you. What the hell are you doing in that ridiculous get-up? I could have blown you to kingdom come." The first guy climbed off me, and the second released my wrists. I got my first good look at their faces. The one who'd hidden in the car was Billy Switzer, a defenseman for the Rockies. The other was a wing, Don Kennit. They helped me to my feet. I looked at the taxi. Mike St. Martin, another defensive player, had the poor cab driver flattened over the hood, a 22-caliber target pistol thrust against the nape of his neck.

"Let him go, Mike," I said. The driver, ashen-faced and trembling like a gerbil, was so shook he could hardly raise himself off the hood. I reached into my wallet and pulled out a twenty-dollar bill. "Sorry, mister—case of mistaken identity. This is all for you if you promise not to say a word to anyone," I said with a paternal pat on the shoulder.

"No one," he reassured me with wild gesticulations. "Not even my wife. No one." He jumped into his taxi and lit out of there like an anti-tank missile.

"Back into the house, quick," I urged. "We may have company any second."

"I'll hide in the car again," Billy Switzer said.

"The hell you will," I laughed grimly. "If I'd been one of them, your upholstery would be soaking up your blood this minute." We retreated to the porch and hurtled into the house.

It was a cheaply and conventionally decorated home of the kind I've seen so often I've dubbed it Professional Athlete Modern. Unless a player is a star with a rich, long-term contract, he can't afford to furnish a home with expensive permanent furniture. Had I been blindfolded, I could probably have found my way faultlessly to the matching fake Danish-modern couch and chairs covered in glinty plaid indestructible fabric, the mosaic-inlaid coffee table on spindly legs with large gaudy enamel ashtrays and a grotesque vase of artificial flowers, wall-to-wall carpeting, a sideboard of cheap wood and Formica veneer, and the ubiquitous 21-inch color television measured diagonally. The only question in doubt was the color scheme. In this case, the room was bathed in blue from the last light of day filtering through translucent nylon curtains.

But the item I could not have predicted was Babette Laclede herself.

It was next to tragic that I didn't have time to study her features in a more leisurely fashion but as there was a distinct possibility we were about to be invaded I had to take them in at a glance and impress them on my memory. Hopefully, the lingering image would carry me through the impending crisis and give me a reason to survive it.

The sneering references to her easy morality made by Ellen Boudreau and Paul Beauregard had engendered a fantasy in my mind of a brassy, vulgar woman with teased hair and heavy makeup, a roadhouse waitress type. Rarely has a fantasy landed so wide of the mark.

She was as pretty and natural as a cover girl for Seventeen magazine. Her hair was silky blond and pinned casually atop her head in a great swirl of soft tresses, uncovering a graceful white neck. Her face, totally devoid of makeup and indeed scrubbed like a milkmaid's, was round and wholesome, heavily flecked with freckles. I rushed past her too fast to catch the color of her eyes but their expression was doelike and, like her small soft mouth, they were round with fright. She wore tight faded blue jeans and a red knitted halter over whose heart-shaped top rim swelled the creamy softness of high, firm breasts.

She stared at me with substantial lack of fascination—revulsion is another way I've heard it described. This was due to the black mustachio, Groucho eyebrows, and black woolly sideburns fixed idiotically beneath a head of blond hair. She must have wondered if her savior had escaped from a vaudeville act. It was at this of all moments, with Doomsday perhaps a minute away, that I decided to remove my disguise, confirming my daddy's theory that man's dominant trait is not intelligence but vanity.

I peered out of the living-room window but the blue dusk disclosed no sign of a car. I posted Mike St. Martin

at this window and had no sooner mined away than he
said, "Car, Dave!"

I leaned over his shoulder and squinted through a crack
in the curtains. A black two-door hardtop glided slowly
up the street from the same direction in which I'd come.
It stopped in front of the house, and a dark face, possibly
black—it was hard to tell with night falling fast—peered
out. Then the car continued up the block.

"It's them, I'm pretty sure. They're casing the place.
They should be back in a couple of minutes." I turned to
the others. "Upstairs, Mrs. Laclede," I ordered. Then, "No,
check that. I'd like you to answer the door when they ring.
Can you act natural when they come in?"

She shrugged. "If I have a cigarette."

Paul produced a pack of Kents. She pulled one out
with long, graceful fingers, long nailed but unpolished,
that trembled faintly. She tore the filter off it and Paul lit
it for her. She sucked the smoke deeply into her lungs. In
the light of the match, her eyes had glowed a dark sea blue.

"They'll ask to go through your house. Take them wherever they want to go," I said. "What's the layout upstairs?"

"Two bedrooms and a bathroom," she said with that
silky voice I'd admired over the phone. With her French
accent, the word came out "bassrum." "There's a large
walk-in closet in the master bedroom, a smaller one in the
guest room, and a big linen closet in the hall."

"Good. Don, get in that bedroom closet, the walk-in in the
master bedroom. Billy, in the linen closet. You guys got guns?"

Billy, a squat, barrel-chested boy, opened his lumberjacket to display a small blue automatic. Don grinned and
said, "Wait'll you see this!" He crossed the room and produced a weapon I hadn't noticed leaning against the wall.

"Good Christ! Is that a machine pistol?"

"Uh-huh, Schmeisser. My father smuggled it into the country after the war. It's loaded, but I have no idea if it works. If it does work, it'll cut a man in two with one burst."

"Hell, if it makes a man say 'Uncle,' it works. Now listen, both of you. Two men are coming here and they're going to tear the house apart looking for something, I can't tell you what. When they open the door you're hidden behind, smack 'em in the face with all you got. Don't shoot if you can help it and for God's sake make sure it's not Mrs. Laclede here that you slug. If there's only one, give a shout. Paul, Mike and I will be downstairs and we'll take care of the other."

"Car's back," Mike whispered. "It's going past again but I think they're going to park."

I started issuing instructions to Paul and Mike, but Paul held up his hands. "You still haven't told us what this is all about, Dave. You're asking us to risk our lives and we don't have a clue what we're doing it for."

It was a helluva time to ask, legitimate though his question was, and though I'd anticipated it, I still didn't have an appropriate answer. I didn't want them to know about the script Guy had been writing but I didn't have a convincing lie on hand as an alternative to the truth. I mumbled something about blackmail, which failed to satisfy Paul. His teammates looked at him, waiting for a signal. I began to break into a cold sweat and was about to say something impatient when Babette touched Paul on the arm and looked at him deeply, mouth pouting. "Will you trust me, Paul?"

Something meaningful passed between them and I knew she was drawing on an account she'd established with him. His debt to her must have been steep because the hard-jawed resistance he'd shown me turned to Silly Putty beneath her gaze. I can't say as how I'd have done any different if she'd turned those heartbreaking orbs on me.

"Well…okay," Paul said feebly. He looked at her as if hypnotized, then snapped his head to break the trance. "Billy, Don, upstairs. Mike, take the coat closet."

"No," I said, "that's the first place they'll look. I want to lull them off guard for a few minutes."

"There's a utility closet in the den," Babette said pointing past the kitchen. "Also a storage closet off the stairs to the cellar."

"Mike, take the den closet, I'll take the other," Paul said, hoisting his rifle.

"What does that leave for me?" I asked Babette.

"Well, there's the basement and the attic…"

"No, they're too far from the action. Anything else up here?"

"Mmm. There's a china closet in the dinette. It's tight. You'll have to hold your breath."

"That would be par for the course today, Mrs. Laclede."

"Babette," she corrected, looking at me coolly. I think it was the first time she'd actually noticed me since my buffoon-like entrance. Had I been Quasimodo under the disguise, it would have been an improvement over the other but from her appraisal, I'd have to say I found some favor in her eyes. In the almost total darkness, those eyes were now purple.

"Babette," I repeated rolling the consonants around my lips and teeth. The name had a deliciously sensual quality, very French, like coquette, soubrette, grisette. "Looky here, Babette, can you make these gents feel at home?"

"Yes, I think so," she purred, pronouncing it "seenk."

I touched her arm. "I seenk so, too. A bientôt, whatever that means."

"Shall I turn on some lights?"

"By all means," I said going to the combination kitchen and casual dining area and opening the door to the china closet. It contained half a dozen shelves set back eight or ten inches from the door. These were piled with plates, bowls, saucers, glasses, silver service, copperware, and appliances and utensils. Overhead was suspended a dozen china cups which tinkled on their hooks like bells when I squeezed into the closet. I got out and took them down quickly, laying them at the back of a lower shelf. Then, remembering I had no weapon, I opened the silverware drawer opposite the china closet and removed a nasty-looking saw-toothed carving knife. Then I sucked in my breath and pulled the closet door closed again. But scrunch as I might, I couldn't pull it completely shut. So I held it tightly against my chest and peered through the half-inch crack, listening.

A moment or two later the doorbell chimed. The front door opened and I strained my ears.

"Mrs. Laclede?" The voice was baritone.

"Yes?"

"May we come in?"

"Who are you?" Just the right tone of perplexity and suspicion in Babette's voice.

"We just want to ask you some questions," said the other voice, a tenor but with crude Bronxese overtones.

"I…well, you're in."

"Shut the door, Sid," the baritone said.

"May I ask just what the hell you're doing, pushing your way—"

"We want to discuss the book your husband was writing," said Sid politely.

"Jesus, how many times do I have to tell people, I don't have it."

"Has anyone else been here?" said Baritone, the one I'd

been calling Alan Page.

"Buzzy Chambers came around shortly after Guy died," Babette replied indignantly. "I told him I didn't have it. Then a man named Bolt—"

"Bolt?" snapped Sid. "He's been here?"

"No," said Babette coolly. "He called me from some-where, long distance, this morning. I told him I don't have it. Now you shove your way in here and I'm telling you I don't have it. What the hell is it about this script, anyway?"

"We've been asked to find it, ma'am," said Sid. "If you'll cooperate with us, you won't…you'll be fine."

"Fine?" Babette replied with broad irony. "Well, that's just wonderful. I happen to be perfectly fine now."

"Well, then," said Sid, not without a sense of humor himself, "put it this way, if you cooperate with us, you'll be very fine."

"If I show you around, anywhere you want to look, will that be all right?"

"For starters," said Sid. He uttered the phrase blandly but for me, it had a chillingly ominous note.

"Just don't mess anything up, all right?"

"We have no desire to mess anything up," Sid said. I'd have liked to see his eyes when he said it. If he wasn't looking at Babette's body he was either subhuman or su-perhuman. "Eddie, you go upstairs, I'll look around down here. You got a basement or attic, Mrs. Laclede?"

"Both."

"Uh-huh. Okay, we'll get around to those. This the living room?"

"It would seem that way to an untrained eye," said Ba-bette making me chuckle so hard I rattled some soup-bowls.

The next two minutes were filled with the sounds of drawers being opened and shut, furniture moved, books being taken down from shelves. Over my head, stairs thumped as Eddie—at last, I had a name for him—mounted to the second floor. Apparently, he went first to the guest bedroom, where neither Billy nor Don was ensconced. But I braced myself. It couldn't be long before Eddie proceeded to the master bedroom, whence out popped Don Kennit. I wanted to be able to move fast when Sid rushed to his companion's aid.

I was so absorbed in reckoning my tactics I forgot about Sid, who suddenly appeared at the entrance to the dinette and flicked on the light. "This is where you eat, I guess," he said. Through the crack in the closet door, I noted that his pistol was holstered.

"Another shrewd observation," Babette said, glancing in my direction and maneuvering between the china closet and his line of vision.

He moved into the kitchen where I couldn't see him and I heard the sound of pantry doors opening and closing, a silverware drawer sliding out on rattling rollers, and even the squeaking hinges of the oven door, the broiler, and the utility door of the stove. The man was thorough.

He drifted back into the dining area and suddenly presented me with a golden opportunity as he turned his back to me to open the refrigerator door. Babette instinctively sensed what was going through my mind and stepped aside, making a rolling motion with her hand, like a driver signaling a car behind him to pass. I balled my fists and pounced out of the closet. Had I wanted to use the blade end of my knife, I'd have easily ventilated Sid. Instead, I clubbed him on the base of his skull with the haft, driving his head against the refrigerator door with an awesome thump. Somehow he managed to stay on his feet and turn for a backhand swipe at me with his elbow but he turned into my free fist and met it with his nose. I dropped my knife, grabbed his hair, and boxed his head three more times against the refrigerator door. He slumped to the foot of the door, eyes rolling. I picked up my knife and flashed the blade flat against his gullet.

I peeled my ears. The sound of our scuffle would surely have attracted Eddie but, hopefully, it would also be the signal for Don and Billy to leap out of hiding. I heard the thunder of feet down the stairs and guessed it was Eddie, who must have moved at the very first sound downstairs, too fast for my friends to intercept him. I had no idea if my other friends, Mike or Paul had emerged from their biding places downstairs or not. If not, there was a good possibility I'd be a dead man as soon as Eddie turned the corner and entered the kitchen. Babette plastered herself against the china closet, her halter top strained against her breasts as she held her breath waiting.

There was a final thud as Eddie hit the bottom of the stairs and I kneeled helplessly over Sid, trapped in the narrow confines of the dinette. This was it, for sure.

But then Eddie stopped, unaccountably. No, not un-accountably, he was exercising caution. Having no idea what awaited him when he turned into the doorway, he'd decided to edge up slowly. I could see the snout of his gun nosing into view. I shifted my eyes to Babette. She had reached over her head and pulled a dishtowel down from a rack over her head. Suddenly she flicked it blindly around the frame of the door. Eddie flinched back out of sight. Just as he did, I heard a tremendous thump and a grunt of pain followed by a shot. Sounds of a tussle, blows exchanged, another grunt and a groan. Then, "I got him!" It was Don Kennit. I held my breath in the ensuing silence.

Don poked his head in the door, grinning toothlessly.

"Where are your teeth?" I said.

"I always take them out before a game," he said, pocketing Eddie's gun. "Sonofabitch got downstairs before I could catch him but he backed right the hell into me. I checked him against the boards and Billy double-teamed him." He reached into his pants pocket and produced his bridge, inserting it into his mouth as artlessly as if he were in a locker room after a game. There was the sound of a heavy object being dragged—it was Billy hauling Eddie by the leg into the dinette.

"Two minutes for high-sticking and five for fighting," he said to Don, laughing. "What do we do with this baggage, Mr. Bolt?"

"Just sit on him a minute," I said, reaching into Sid's holster and removing his gun. A moment later Paul and Mike walked in, Mike brandishing that terrifying machine pistol. "Thanks for the help, boys."

"We weren't sure…" Paul started to say but I waved his apology away.

Babette stepped forward, looking at Paul. "At least you can pull this one away from the refrigerator. I want to break out a six-pack of beer."

While Babette and the boys were downing their refreshments, I went to the kitchen phone and dialed 314-555-1212, St. Louis information. I secured Kaleeka's home phone number and called him. He answered the phone with a mouthful of dinner.

"Hello, Mr. Kaleeka, Dave Bolt here."

A long silence punctuated by accelerated chewing and swallowing. "Yeah?"

"Sorry to interrupt your dinner but I got a couple of Care packages for you, one marked Sid and one marked Eddie. What do you want me to do with them?"

"Are they dead or alive?" he rasped.

"Alive—at the moment." I looked down and noticed their eyes rolling and limbs twitching as consciousness filtered back into their brains.

"Shoot them in the head," Kaleeka said.

"Sorry, that's not my style but I'll be glad to castrate them. And that goes for anybody else you send around."

He mulled for a moment, then said calmly, "Listen, Bolt, two men don't mean shit to me. I can raise more troops than the Chinese army. You just remember what I told you in the car. I want that book, and you're not going to pass a restful night until I have it. That's all I got to say to you." He emphasized this declaration with a slam of the phone.

I looked down at my captives again. Eddie's eyes were open and bleary but fearful. "You were putting Mr. Kaleeka on about castrating us," he said. His voice had a downward inflection as if he was afraid of making it a question.

I kneeled down, unzipped his trousers, and pressed the blade of my knife against the bulge between his legs. "I don't know, it all depends. How much do you like your balls, Eddie?"

"Enough to haul them onto the next plane to St. Louis," he said.

I smiled. "Mrs. Laclede was right, you're a man of rare perception. My friends will escort you to the airport."

CHAPTER VII

· · · ·

"Are you hungry?" Babette asked, squatting to sponge some blood smears off the kitchen floor where Eddie had shed a negligible amount of his life fluid.

"No, but some coffee would do real fine."

"I have instant only, if you don't mind."

"That'll suit me perfectly."

Seated at the dinette table, I watched her move lithely around the kitchen, stretching for the jar of instant coffee, kneeling before the refrigerator hunting for a can of evaporated milk, bending over the silverware drawer. She had the grace of a dancer and she knew it, casting sidelong glances at me as she performed her domestic chores to see if I was looking and appreciating. I was both, abundantly.

"You are much more attractive without your disguise," she said, "but you left some of it on your face. Hold still." She got down a bottle of cleaning fluid and a rag and stood over me, dissolving the remnants of paste and black hair clinging to my upper lip, eyebrows and sideburns, but affording me at the same time the vista of the crescents of her breasts. Her perfume was delicate but mingled with a not unpleasant odor of sweat, the product of the fear and tension of the last hour. She knew she was titillating me, though her chatter was as superficial as a professional barber's. I twisted my fingers agonizingly in my lap. I would look but I must not touch. I had business to conduct with her and my objectivity tends to dissolve in vaginal fluids.

"There." She rinsed the residue off with soap and water and stepped away to look at me like a painter addressing his canvas. "Yes, a very nice face. I like the hair, tightly curled like Lord Byron's."

"Lord Byron couldn't run a post pattern," I said.

"Pardon?" She pronounced it "pah-do." I liked her accent.

"Nothing. Just feeling a little silly. I always get that way after narrowly escaping death. You got any cookies? I'm a little hungry after all."

She got a box of Oreos out of the pantry and I munched some while she poured hot water out of a kettle into the brown nuggets of freeze-dried Maxwell House at the bottom of our china cups. The coffee foamed into life and I drank mine at a temperature too hot to support life on this planet. The brew went down beautifully and I lit a cigar. Babette smoked a cigarette and we shared a tranquil moment, the first I'd had all day. Then I took up the cudgels.

"Do you mind talking about Guy?"

"No," she said with a shrug. "Life goes on."

"What kind of man was he?"

"A good man, good-natured. He liked people. He made few enemies, even on the ice."

"That's not the impression I get from his script. He struck me as a man with a chip on his shoulder."

"When he wrote the book, he had one. He'd been given the shitty end of the stick."

I smiled at her forthright use of the idiom. "You mean at Chicago."

"Yes. They punished him for losing. That was contemptible."

"Him and Ned Boudreau, you mean."

Her eyes flickered. "Yes, and Ned Boudreau, of course," she said, almost as if she'd forgotten. An impression registered on me but I couldn't name it and didn't know what to do with it.

"Do you feel there might have been another reason for them to fire Guy? I know a lot of folks out there were bitter about their home team losing that playoff but canning the goalies—that's pretty excessive."

"The only reason I can think of is that they were getting old, at least in terms of professional sports. Guy was thirty-four, Ned was a year or two younger. Maybe the management saw this as an opportunity to release them."

"I don't know. They say goalies get better with age. Bill Durnan, one of the greatest goalies who ever lived, started when he was twenty-eight and won the Vezina Trophy six times in the next seven years. So I don't buy that. And no management is so vindictive it will can a goalie, or two in this case, who brings them to the playoffs."

"There were politics, you know. The mayor—"

"I know all about that but it still doesn't make sense to me. No, I'm talking about...oh, you know. Something funny." She knit her eyebrows. "Something crooked," I said bluntly.

She looked into her coffee cup, then lit another cigarette. Her reaction was so mild that the blazing look of scorn she suddenly leveled at me caught me completely off guard. "How could you dare to say that?"

"Easy, woman, easy. I'm just trying to get to the bottom of this thing."

"Guy was no more capable of throwing a game than… than…" She searched for a comparison and gave up, waving her hand in disgust. "And that goes for Ned, too."

"How well did you know Ned?" I asked, looking for the same response she'd displayed a minute earlier. But this time I got only a fisheye.

"I knew him, that's all," she said with a shrug. "No better than I knew other players on Guy's teams."

"How well was that?" It was a cruel question but it needed asking.

Her eyes narrowed to a deadly squint. "Who's been telling you tales? I'll bet it's that bitch Ellen Boudreau. And I introduced her to Ned, too. That's gratitude for you."

I held up my hands. "Look, Babette, I'm not interested in your character except as far as it may pertain to Guy's death and the disappearance of that script." I gave her a minute to cool down and said, "How about looking at it from the viewpoint of an objective investigator? That's me." I chomped on my cigar.

She threw an arm over her chair and watched me warily. "Go on."

"Guy is writing this book. In it, he promises to blow the top off a gambling scandal. He's killed in a car accident. Does that say anything to you?"

"Nothing that hasn't been said to me already."

"Morty Kaleeka, a professional gambler with Mafia connections, gets wind that Guy was writing a book and sends two torpedoes to shake you and your place upside down to find it. Does that say anything to you?"

"Not yet, but keep talking."

"I spoke to a hockey player this morning who told me that if a game was going to be thrown, the likeliest player to do it would be the goalie. And the likeliest time would be the playoffs, when betting action runs high. Now, how fine a point do I have to put on all this?"

She ruminated over the gray smoke of her cigarette, which had burned down to a stub between her long fingers. "I still can't believe those boys would do such a thing."

"Did either of them have money troubles at the time?"

"No more than any other hockey player."

"Did either of them show signs, after the playoff, of having, let's say, a surplus of money? I mean, did they buy anything they couldn't ordinarily afford?"

She reflected a few seconds. "I can't speak for Ned but as for Guy, definitely not. In fact, when Denver hired him, he had to draw an advance to move there."

"Did you keep Guy's bank books after he died?"

"Savings passbooks, you mean? We didn't have a savings account. We never saved anything. I went over his accounts, such as they were, when the lawyers settled the estate. I found just what you'd expect. Nothing. In fact, I still owe twelve hundred dollars for his funeral."

"What do you do for money?" I asked her.

"His life insurance will carry me for a year or so but I've been looking for a job."

"Can we talk about the script?"

She sighed. "Yes. Yes, I suppose, if you must."

"Were you aware he was working on it?"

"Yes, but he didn't tell me what was in it and wouldn't allow me to see it. The first I ever saw of it was after Guy died, when Buzzy Chambers showed me the first few chapters and the—how would you say?—résumé of what was to come."

"Where did Guy work when he was writing?"

"In the guest bedroom. He had a little portable typewriter."

"And you never went in there when he was away?"

"Oh, yes. I would not be human if I wasn't curious. But he hid it. I think he even carried it with him when he went out." I started to raise an obvious question but she cut it off with a slash of her hand. "Don't bother, Buzzy searched Guy's locker and found nothing. He had no safe deposit box that I know of, at least I found no key in his effects."

"Did he make carbon copies of what he wrote?"

"*Sais pas*". Buzzy examined Guy's desk after the funeral. He found typing paper but no carbon paper. I doubt if Pierre made copies. He had enough difficulty typing the... how would you say?"

"The original?"

"Yes, the original. Maybe he made copies on a copy machine, I just don't know."

I tapped the table with my fingertips.

"No more questions?" she asked.

"Not for the moment. You look disappointed."

"I suppose I am. It means you'll be leaving."

"You don't want me to leave?"

"Not yet, really. I'm still very shook-up. In fact, if you didn't interpret it wrongly, I would ask you to stay the night. I could put you up in the guest room." She looked at me levelly and I knew she was in earnest.

"I don't think so. I wouldn't be happy alone in a house with you, knowing you're only a wall away." I reached out for her hand.

The contact seemed to ignite her. Her arm shuddered and I could see the blond filaments of hair on her forearm stand up. I rose from my seat, put my hand on that irresistible stretch of neck exposed by her upswept hair, and kissed her. Her kiss was hot and hungry and her nails dug into the back of my scalp. Then her lips went ice cold and she pushed me away. "They told you I'm easy."

I withheld a reply. It wasn't her easiness that attracted me but her intrinsic sensuality. I didn't think she'd believe that.

"I'm merely lonely, that's all," she said. "And I like men. Is there anything wrong with that?"

"Not from my viewpoint."

"I'm not indiscriminate. I'm not a whore."

"Nobody said any such thing."

"You assumed I would go to bed with you."

"I assume everybody will. I'm very egotistical," I laughed.

She looked at me with an expression that changed, like patterns of sunlight and shadow on a day when clouds scud rapidly across the sun, from cynicism to suspicion to amusement to coyness. I wished I could trace the thought process that precipitated these changes but they traveled too fast. Besides, the important thing was the product of these emotional leaps. "You're very nice, Dave," she said, caressing my face. "Come upstairs and lay me."

I gulped, almost not crediting my ears. Apparently, she had needed only the flimsiest excuse to establish her honor then she could accede to seduction without a further pang of guilt.

Well, I didn't pretend to understand it but I'm not one to look gift horses in the mouth or any other orifice for that matter. I took her hand again and led her up the stairs and into the bedroom. She disappeared into the bathroom for a minute. In the light of the hallway indirectly illuminating the room, I looked around. It was a very feminine room, pink and ruffly with a gaily printed bedspread, matching café curtains and wall-to-wall carpet, a velvet chair piled with cushions, and porcelain figurines. I suspect the room had been this way even while Guy was alive and the burly goalie must have felt faintly unmanned in it.

I looked at the closed bathroom door, fascinated by the shadows that streamed out of the crack beneath it. At last it opened and Babette emerged, garbed only in a pair of flowered bikini panties. When it came to sex, this was obviously a lady who didn't fart around. She stood before me, head tilted and lips pouting, arms held out like a dancer's, legs close together with one knee jutting in front of the other, inviting me to admire her body.

There was nothing to find fault with. Her long neck flowed into slender shoulders which sloped to a pair of high breasts of medium size, with light pink nipples lying flat against the flesh. Her waist was narrow but flared in gentle parabolas into beautifully sculptured hips. Her legs were long and perfectly tapered, not muscular but firm and sleek, haloed in blond peach-fuzz backlit by the bathroom light.

I stood against the dresser taking this vision in. She was almost too beautiful to befoul with my grimy paws, but this wave of romantic idealism subsided quickly—it took, I should say, about one ten-thousandth of a second.

I stepped against her and touched my lips to that neck that was, despite all her other fine attributes, the most compelling thing about her body. She shuddered, and goose-bumps suddenly dappled her flesh. I kissed her shoulders, then her breasts, maneuvering tauntingly around her nipples. Her perfume intoxicated me and increased the ardor of my kisses. Her chest rose and fell with growing excitement, and she twisted her shoulders urging her nipples into my mouth. I could no longer stay away from them. I took one into my mouth and moiled it with my tongue. "Ahh," she sighed, leaning on my shoulders for support. Then she pushed my head down to her belly.

I reached behind her and slid my hands underneath the waistband of her silk panties to cup her buttocks. They were fight and firm, and they dimpled as she pulled taut their muscles. I squeezed the flesh and pressed my lips against her belly. She emitted a kind of singing sound and pushed my head even lower. I rubbed my cheek against the soft mound above her crotch. Her hips undulated, bringing her fragrant pubic region maddeningly close to my tongue.

I pulled her panties down and she stepped out of them. Then I returned my face to that deliciously aromatic area the poets have named the Mound of Venus, silkily vege-tated with blond hair. She parted her legs and I thrust my lips and tongue into the sweet soft depths of her. Her knees trembled, then buckled, and she lay down on the carpet. "Take off your clothes," she pleaded.

It was not a difficult request to comply with. I executed it in a little less time than it takes Mercury Morris to get to the outside.

She put her hand on my leg in explicit invitation. I stretched out beside her, my head against her thighs, my thighs beside her head. "Lovely," she murmured, taking my painfully hard member into her mouth. I felt an aching rush of desire in my bowels as she clamped her nails into my but-tocks and drew me full into her. Maybe she was no whore, but she was as highly skilled an amateur as I'd ever want to know. She seemed to have made a painstaking survey of the sensitive areas of a man's body and managed to find them as quickly and accurately as an acupuncturist. For a moment I almost lost control, and forced my mind to distract itself with such irrelevancies as hockey and Oreo cookies to prevent a premature release. At last I regained control and pressed soul kisses far into that hot moist cavity of hers until her hips were churning faster and her sighs, muffled by the swollen organ in her mouth, came louder and louder.

I moved to disengage from her so that I could climb astride her, but she whimpered No and clasped me even tighter, sucking me with deeper ardor yet. And that was it for me. Moments later a stupendous convulsion came roaring out of my insides, followed by one in her own. I could feel her spasms around my tongue as she writhed beneath me like a snake pinned to the ground. Our climax seemed never-ending. We came and came and came like a pair of long, slow-moving freight trains gliding endlessly past one another. By the time the last twitch of pleasure subsided I felt as cleansed as a well-scrubbed milk pail.

"That was good," she panted, rolling away, "to begin with."

It was then I knew I was in for a heavy night.

CHAPTER VIII

• • • •

It was a considerably wasted Dave Bolt who stood the following morning on the observation deck of Mile High Airport watching Babette Laclede board the Air Canada flight to Winnipeg, where she'd arranged to stay with her sister until the danger was past. She was so demure in her mousy brown linen suit that I could make almost no connection between the figure ascending the steps to the plane's door and the primitive animal who had occupied me until six in the morning with her insatiable lust. I'd, at last, had to pull her off me so I could get an hour of sleep and when I awoke, I was looking into her eyes. "I'm ready," she breathed, touching me tentatively between the legs.

Although she'd drained me of emotion, I was still able to summon a twinge of pity for her late husband, on whose head she'd undoubtedly stuck more horns than you can find in the King Ranch corrals at roundup time.

Now she had paused at the top of the steps to blow me a kiss. I raised my hand and waggled my fingers, a major effort.

I went to the coffee shop and consumed a herculean breakfast, double portions of everything from juice, coffee,

steak and eggs and toast to apple pie and even Jell-O. A
grandmotherly waitress clucked at me approvingly and the
cash register gal kept looking past me wondering where the
other six diners in my party were. She couldn't believe I'd
consumed all that food by myself. But I guess I'd used up
enough calories in the last eight hours to heat Fairbanks,
Alaska, for a week.

I went to a phone booth and called Vincent Sturdevant
in Montreal to report on the eventful days since he'd asked
me to undertake his investigation. I told him about everything but the bout in Babette's bedroom which he would
not have condoned even if he believed it.

After I'd run everything down, he ruminated silently,
then said, "So what you're suggesting is that this Kaleeka
bought one of the Chicago goalies—or maybe both of
them—and fixed the playoffs."

"Yes, that's what the evidence points to. But he didn't
know about Guy's book."

He ignored this last information.

"Which one do you think it was, Dave?"

"I don't know. As I recall, Guy Laclede was the goalie
in three of the four losing games so that would strongly
suggest it was he. But then I ask myself, why would he
expose himself in his own book? If he was going to report
a scandal, wouldn't it be somebody else's?"

"That makes sense. You think, then, it may have been
Ned Boudreau?"

"Uh-huh."

There was another silence, heavy and sad. He punctuated it with clucks of pity. "You don't think Ellen knew
about it, do you?"

"Hell, no! Do you think she'd have commissioned a
book if she thought that was going to turn up in it?"

"Jesus, that poor girl. When she finds out…"

"Well, let's not jump to conclusions. I want to talk to Ned Boudreau first. Do you have a copy of the NHL schedule? Where are the Sabres playing today?"

There was a pause and the sound of papers shuffling. "Philadelphia. They return to Buffalo tomorrow for their last game of the season."

"Okay, that's where I'm heading next. Now, there's one more person I want to talk to, so can you tell me what happened to Irv Staley, the Black Hawk coach, after Chicago fired him?"

"He's at the University of Wisconsin, coaching their hockey team. Just a second." Another pause, more rattling of paper as he searched for Staley's address and phone number. He read them to me and I was just about to hang up when something occurred to me, something I'd stupidly overlooked and which now came back to me with devastating force. "Whoo boy!"

"What's the matter, Dave?"

"I just realized if Ned Boudreau is implicated in this scandal, Kaleeka may be going after him next. We've got to warn him."

"My God, you're right. You'd better call him right away."

"I don't think Ned would appreciate the call coming from me, after our rumble the other night. Would you mind doing it from there?"

"Sure. You realize, though, that by calling Ned, we're tipping him off that we know—or at least we suspect—what he did in Chicago."

"Yes, but we'll have to take that chance, Mr. Sturdevant. If Kaleeka bumps him off, the case is closed."

"Unless that manuscript turns up."

"Unless that manuscript turns up," I repeated with a sinking hunch that it never would. "Tell Ned to be extremely cautious until I can get to Philadelphia. I'll call you from there."

I left the booth and checked at the ticket counters on flights to Philadelphia. There were no direct ones, but a fairly fast one with only two stops left in an hour and a half, giving me time for some more phone calls.

I went back to the bank of booths and placed a person-to-person call to Irv Staley at the University of Wisconsin. After a five-minute manhunt at the Athletic Department, Staley came to the phone. I'd never met him but knew from pictures of him that he was a moon-faced, middle-aged man who'd played a year or two without distinction for the Black Hawks before the war and afterwards had climbed the beanstalk of farm-club coaching positions until tapped by the parent club. He was a better coach than he'd been a player but unfortunately less of a politician than he'd been a coach. When the management and half the city of Chicago had railroaded him, Guy Laclede, and Ned Boudreau off the Black Hawks, he'd proved incapable of fighting back. He'd simply shrugged, asserted he'd done the best he could, accepted full responsibility for the Black Hawks' defeat by the Rangers, begged the management not to let go of the goalies, and stole silently away.

"The name is Bolt," I said. "I'm kind of a minister without portfolio for the NHL and thought I might drop in on you to discuss something."

"What specifically, Mr. Bolt?" His voice was Midwest Engineer, friendly but businesslike, but there was a touch of caution in it, too.

"I'd prefer to explain when I get there," I said.

"I'm sorry. I have to pin you down now," he insisted. It was obvious he knew.

"It's about the events surrounding your dismissal from Chicago."

"I've said all I'm going to say on that subject. You'd be wasting your time."

"I'm being paid for that."

"Then you'd be wasting mine and I'm not being paid for that."

"Why are you so reluctant to speak about it?"

"Wouldn't you be?"

"You may have to speak about it to a grand jury if you don't speak to me," I said.

The gambit achieved its desired effect. There was a tremor in his voice When, after a pause, he asked, "Why would a grand jury be called into it?"

I kept up the shock tactics. "Come on, Irv, you know why. Some evidence has surfaced that the last round of that playoff series was thrown by one of your goalies, maybe both."

Another pause and a sighed "What do you want to know?"

"Well, how about the truth?"

"There is no truth. You can look at the videotapes of that series from now till Doomsday, you'll never know for sure."

"But one might suspect, is that what you're saying?"

"One might. I did not but they did."

"They—the front office of Chicago, you mean?"

"Yes."

"What did they suspect?"

"I'm sure you've figured that out. Guy and Ned alternated at goal. Guy lost Games One, Three, and Five, Ned won Games Two, Four, and Six, and lost only one, the final. Guy Laclede had never lost three consecutive games in all his years as a pro."

"So they suspected Laclede, then," I said.

"Yes, but they had enough suspicion of Boudreau to release him, too."

"Why?"

"Have you seen the video tapes?"

"No."

"See them."

"Can't you tell me?"

"I'd rather not," Staley said. "I'd like to know what conclusions you come to from screening the tapes. How well do you know hockey?"

"I'm not a maven," I said, utilizing a word Trish had taught me.

"A what?"

"That's Yiddish for 'expert,'" I said.

"Funny, you don't sound Jewish. Well, have a 'maven' by your side when you screen them."

"Okay, but none of this explains why you were canned," I said and the odd thing is that even as I said it, the answer came to me.

Staley confirmed my hunch. "Because they suspected me, too, don't you see? They thought I was in on the fix. They thought I'd actually put it in."

"Why would they think that?"

"I'd…rather not say."

His resistance only spurred me on. I was very excited now, like a wildcatter boring into a stratum of hard rock knowing that when he penetrates it, he'll tap oil. "Is it because you were in on the fix?"

"Of course not." His comeback was almost too spontaneous and forceful. At any rate, I was not satisfied.

"Then why," I pressed, "would they think you'd been involved in a fix?"

"Because…because I'd been known to put a bet down from time to time."

I could hardly contain myself. My shafts had thumped into the target closer and closer to the bullseye. Now I nocked my best arrow, sighted carefully on the center, and released. "With a man named Kaleeka, perhaps?"

"I…" The truth has a strange fascination for a guilty man. He could have hung up but it apparently never occurred to him to do so. "Yes. But listen to me, Bolt, please," he whined. "Kaleeka approached me with a proposition. It was a golden opportunity but I turned it down. I bet with him to supplement my income, that's all, but I would never go that far, even if it meant a king's ransom." I didn't know whether or not to believe him but I let him talk. "I told him nothing doing but he said, 'That's okay. There are some people on your team who don't have your scruples.' He didn't tell me who they were but as the playoffs progressed it was pretty easy to see who Kaleeka must have had in mind."

"Laclede?"

"Yes. And yet, you look at those tapes…" His voice trailed off.

"Does the name Napolitani mean anything to you?" I asked.

"I think," Staley said, "at this point, I'd better consult with my lawyer."

"You know something? I think that's a very good idea," I replied. "But do yourself a favor. If you've been lying to me—if you were in on the fix I suggest you hightail it out of where you are until this investigation is over, because Kaleeka may just decide to silence anyone who was involved."

"He already did."

"Laclede?"

I decided to let him believe Kaleeka had killed Laclede. Let Staley worry. It might flush the whole truth out if there was any left to flush. "Yes, Laclede."

"Well," Staley said with a hollow righteousness, "I have nothing to hide. I've told you the God's honest truth. But —maybe I'll take a short sabbatical anyway."

CHAPTER IX

· · · ·

I made one more call. I'd been out of touch with my office for close to a week and it was time to see what catastrophes had occurred in my absence.

Actually, I didn't believe that. Trish was the soul of competence, and my new assistant, Dennis Whittle, could only strengthen my confidence that I could spend a week away without worrying. Which is why the ensuing conversation left me in a towering dudgeon.

"Red Dog Sports Management," said the voice at the other end of the line. It belonged to Dennis, and its quality was harried and petulant.

"Dennis, that you?"

"Dave! Where the fuck have you been? I've been chasing you over half the North American continent."

I looked at the earpiece of the phone. "That's no way to speak to your boss," I said, half-jokingly. If I hadn't sensed genuine desperation in his voice, I'd have withered him for talking to me that way.

"My ex-boss, you mean."

"Huh?"

"I've quit, buddy. I'm just sitting here holding down the shop till you get back, then it's goodbye and good luck."

"Hold it, hold it, hold it! What's going on? Where's Trish?"

"Ah, Trish, Trish. Yes, I seem to recall there is someone on your payroll who goes by that name."

"Where is she, Dennis?"

"She's not here."

"Obviously, she's not there."

"She's never here, man. She's never here and she is never here."

"Where the hell is she?"

"Out playing agent."

"Whoo boy," I groaned, pounding the coin box. "You want to start from the beginning?"

"You haven't enough coin to hear it from the beginning."

"I'm on credit card."

He took a deep breath. "Okay. I started Monday, right?"

"Right."

"Right. So Monday morning I get here and she says, 'I don't know if Dave told you but I'm no longer a secretary. I'm an assistant. That means you and I are on equal footing. We're both going to be doing the office work and we're both going to be handling clients.' Did you tell her that, Dave?"

"Forget what I told her for the moment. Go on."

"All right. So I said to myself, if that's what Dave said, that's cool. She starts showing me the ropes, you know, the file system, the phones, the client list, the bookkeeping system, the whole bit. So far, so good. I figure, it's a small office, we've both got to pitch in. Then she says, 'Dave gave me a special assignment just before he left. He wants me to procure some female clients for the agency, more women athletes.' You told her that?"

I clutched the phone with white-knuckled anger. "Go on."

"Next thing I know, she takes off, leaving me holding the bag. And baby, the secretary's bag is not my bag, you dig? I mean, it is one big fucking—"

"She's been gone ever since?"

"No, every once in a while she breezes in, looks at the mail and phone messages, tells me how to handle them, and takes off on another appointment."

I choked and sputtered.

"You want a complete description of the chaos?" Dennis asked. "Or shall I condense it for you?"

"I can imagine."

"Uh-uh. A man with the imagination of a Tolkien could not begin to grasp what's been going on in this office. These telephones, for instance. Would you like a list of the clients and eminent celebrities I have cut off by pushing the wrong buttons?"

"I think I'm going to cry," I said.

"I got so desperate, I called this temporary agency for a secretary? They sent this chick, she was slightly heavier than Willis Reed, only she was slightly shorter than Ernie DiGregorio. She said she was dieting, so all she ate was prune whip yogurt—five tons of it in one afternoon. She typed with her shoulders, or maybe it was her knees. Her telephone voice sounded like the possessed kid in The Exorcist. If the purple fingerprints on your files put you in mind of prune whip yogurt, that's what they are. And now for the bad news…hold on, there's the other phone."

He punched Hold, only it wasn't Hold. The next thing I heard was a dial tone.

I called him back. "Hello, yeah, what?" he shouted.

"It's me again."

"Jesus, I thought I'd lost you. Another week waiting for you to show up—I couldn't endure it. Anyway, that was

Vince Sturdevant who just called. He said if you should phone in soon, to call him right away and do not go to Philadelphia. Dave, what's going on?"

"I'll call you back after I speak to him. Look, Dennis, try to keep calm a little longer."

He sighed. "Okay. Situation desperate but not serious."

"And if Trish shows up, you tell her she's to stay there."

"She doesn't strike me as the kind of girl anyone can tell anything."

"Fuck her."

"Not without a full suit of armor," he sighed.

CHAPTER X

· · · ·

I stayed in the phone booth, taking deep breaths to regain my composure. I suspected I'd need it when I called Vince Sturdevant. And I was right.

"Bad news," he said.

"We're too late," I guessed.

"Yes. Ned Boudreau's disappeared. Hasn't shown up in two games. It'll be in the afternoon papers. Nobody has a clue."

"God, why didn't I think of this earlier?" I'd made more mistakes than the Mets had made in their first five seasons. "Have you called Ellen? Maybe she knows where he is."

"Ellen doesn't know but she said she wanted to talk to you as soon as possible."

"That gives me two reasons to catch the next plane to New York," I said.

That was the eleven-a.m. flight, and I spent four dark hours on that sonofabitch brooding on the condition of life which, I found decidedly nasty, short, brutish, and poor. I disdained lunch and sat curled around more booze than is good for me, contemplating a long list of people I'd have cheerfully murdered. The list ended with myself. I squirmed so much in my seat I developed saddle sores. From time to time I groaned aloud, alarming the pimply-faced pre-med student next to me until he vacated his seat and spent the rest of the flight smoking nervously outside the galley.

With the time change, it was close to six when I arrived at the Lincoln Building but I went to my office anyway, having told Dennis to stay there until I showed up.

I had no sooner stepped off the elevator than the shouting reached my ears. I hustled down the corridor, then stopped with my hand on my office door, listening.

"That's not what he told me he told you," Dennis was yelling.

"Then either he's lying or you are," Trish shot back.

"You know, if you weren't a broad I'd say something—"

"Yeah and if you weren't a spade, I'd say something to you, buster. In fact, I'll say it anyway. You're a big dumb asshole. Anyone who could fuck up calls on a two-line telephone hasn't enough brains to fill a termite's snatch. How you survived in the fucking American Basketball Association—Dave!"

I stood in the doorway, trying to make sense of the scene. Dennis and Trish were squared off with only the width of the receptionist's desk separating them. Dennis brandished a rolled-up magazine, Trish one of my football trophies. The desk itself looked like a direct hit on a stationery store. Beyond the reception room, unfilled file folders were stacked to vertiginous heights or flung at random on the floor, contents spilled out like the gutted remnants of a once-crack military brigade. A spool of black typewriter ribbon trailed out of one typewriter, winding its way across the room and terminating under the radiator. My Pitney-Bowes postage machine had been placed on the floor for some incomprehensible reason and beside it was my checkwriting machine with six checks arranged around it like a fan.

My eyes returned to the reception room and I felt sick. On my nice powder-blue rug, resembling a squid squashed beneath a hobnail boot, was a hideous purple stain. It could only have been dried prune whip yogurt.

"Dave," Trish cried again. "Am I ever glad to see you!"

"Glad? When I'm through with you, you'll be lucky to walk to the unemployment office under your own power."

Her jaw dropped and she looked at me with eyes filled with hurt. "Well, if that doesn't suck!"

"Do you hear the mouth on this broad?" Dennis pleaded.

"I know all about her mouth."

"I've been in ghetto riots, I never heard even black chicks talk like that," he said, shaking his head.

"Sucks, is what it does," Trish repeated, also shaking her head.

As long as everybody was shaking his head, I shook mine, too. "I can't believe this. I really can't."

Trish pointed a finger at Dennis. "Do you know what this man—?"

"Sit down," I told her.

"Where's to sit? He's piled papers all over the—"

"SIT FUCKING DOWN!"

I don't think I'd ever spoken to her that way. But she'd never provoked me so thoroughly, either. Looking at me like a cornered bunny, she plopped into the chair behind her desk.

"First time she's sat in that chair all week," Dennis chuckled.

"You sit down, too."

He removed an assortment of documents from the visitor's couch and lowered himself onto it.

I turned to Trish. "Now, would you like to explain where you've been and what you've been doing?"

"Oh," she singsonged, "just bringing in half a dozen clients whose total earnings can be expected to reach half a million dollars this year, including endorsements."

I pretended not to hear what she'd said. "On company time?"

She stared. "Company time, shmompany time, what the hell difference does that make?"

"This is the difference," I said. I prodded a nondescript pile of papers perched like an inverted pyramid atop her desk. It collapsed, half the papers sliding into her lap.

She looked at Dennis. "Can you believe this man? I line up fifty thousand dollars in commissions and he's complaining about a messy desk."

"I did not authorize you to abandon your post to go chasing all over hell-and-gone looking for clients."

"I did not abandon my post," she snorted, breathing defiance and glaring at me with fulminating eyes. "I left it in the hands of your new assistant. How was I supposed to know his hands had six thumbs each?"

"Yeah," replied Dennis, shaking his finger at her, "and I'm gonna shove all twelve up your—"

"THAT'S ENOUGH!" I shouted again. Then the weight of the last few days pressed like a thousand atmospheres on my shoulders. I leaned heavily against the desk. I thought my knees were going out from under me. "Please," I whimpered, "enough."

They rose simultaneously to offer support. It was the first thing they'd done together all week long.

"I'll get him some water," Dennis said.

"He takes bourbon when he's like this," Trish replied superciliously, rushing to the bar in my office. Dennis led me to the couch. Trish returned with my bourbon and branch water. Anxiously they watched me sip it.

"Now," said Trish, "what the hell have you been doing?"

The alcohol revitalized me, dissolving my furor. I summarized the Laclede case for them, then remembered something. "Did you reach Ellen Boudreau?" I asked Dennis.

"Yes, she's at home waiting for your call."

"You want to get her for me? Tell her to meet me in fifteen minutes at—oh, anywhere—January's. That's at First Avenue and Seventy-eighth."

He burrowed through a ream of memos, invoices, contracts, and what appeared to be the cardboard container of a Big Mac until he found the paper with Ellen's number on it. While he dialed, Trish was looking at me, sober and ashamed. "I'm sorry, Dave, I've let you down. I guess I got carried away."

"Who are these phenomenal females you've gotten?"

She brightened. "Well, there's Liz Breamer, for one."

I raised my eyebrows. Liz was a hot young tennis star who'd upset Billie Jean King and Chris Evert at Wimbledon before losing the final to Yvonne Goolagong. Right afterwards, she'd turned pro. "How'd you manage to accomplish that?"

"I'm good, that's all. But I've always told you that."

"Who else?"

"Bobbi Bostwick, Ann-Marie Boulez, Martha Mc-Givern, Jody Sloan, and Renee Valdez. And stop trying to look nonchalant. I know you're impressed."

"I'll be more impressed when I see how you manage them."

"I'm not worried. I've done my homework. I've studied at the feet of the Master." She looked at me with adoration.

"Master still wants to kick Disciple in teeth," I said.

"You'll get over it. Especially when you hear who I'm working on."

"Working on?"

"Going after—as a client."

"I don't want to hear."

Dennis hung up the phone. "Ellen will be at January's

in fifteen minutes."

"Good. Now, can we all have a nice, calm, reasonable, mature discussion?"

They looked at me expectantly, if a little anxiously.

"I'm afraid," I said, trying not to sound like a preacher, "I've been remiss in laying out the Table of Organization around here, for which I apologize. This is a very small, young outfit. Maybe someday we'll own fifteen floors of the World Trade Center and we'll have a thousand employees in fifty categories of specialization. But right now, there's you two and me, makes three, and a lot of work. So we all have to pitch in."

"Right on," said Dennis, looking at Trish.

"Absolutely," said Trish, looking at Dennis.

"Dennis, I hired you to be my assistant, but I never meant for you to do only glamour jobs. You're going to have to master secretarial skills. That may seem demeaning or even unmanning, though in this day and age men are doing everything women do except give birth, and I'm told they're working on that, too."

"I'd rather be in labor for eight hours than operate those button telephones. They are perverse!" he whistled.

I turned to Trish. "Trish, I hate to admit it, but you've won your point. You deserve to be more than a secretary." She beamed and looked triumphantly at Dennis but before she could gloat I said, "But until we can afford another employee, you're still my secretary. I don't care how much fine work you do outside, it's negated if you leave this place in the disgraceful condition it's in now."

I rose tiredly. Trish had tears in her eyes. Dennis looked so remorseful he made a bloodhound look arrogant. "I may have to leave town again right away but the next time I walk into this office, I want to see it the same way it was the last time I left it. Especially that!" I pointed to the purple stain in the carpet.

"I don't know if that'll come out," Dennis said, toeing it. It was hard and crusty.

"Even if you have to lick it off, I want it out."

I taxied over to January's, a dark but pleasant restaurant on the upper East Side, catering to the young and hip and, occasionally, some ballplayers. Although the place was jammed, I knew we wouldn't be disturbed and probably not even noticed, for there was a television in the bar and folks were jammed twelve deep to watch Boston and Philadelphia locking horns in first-round NBA Eastern Conference Playoff action. As Ellen hadn't arrived yet, I sidled up to the edge of the throng and watched. It was a sloppy and ragged contest, but for me, for whom missing playoffs is like a Muslim missing Mecca, the five brief minutes I watched were like ambrosia.

Then Ellen arrived and I pulled myself away. She wore a shoulderless red dress that made her raven hair even blacker. Her eyes were red-rimmed and tired, find she lit up a Winchester nervously the moment she stepped into the restaurant. "I'm glad to see you," she said, enclosing my hand with hers. Hers was cold and the pressure of her fingers inconsequential, a formality. She was abstracted.

"You hungry?" I asked. "I didn't eat on the plane. They got great seafood here."

"Maybe I could use a burger or something. I haven't eaten all day myself."

We took a table in the glass-enclosed sidewalk annex and watched the parade of quietly desperate young people passing by while we waited for our orders.

"Did you see the item in the Post?" she asked.

"No, I haven't had a chance to look at a paper."

She reached into her purse and pulled out a clipping. "It says Ned took a leave of absence."

"Is that true?"

"Of course not, it's nonsense. I called Coach Richard in Philadelphia. He said Ned hadn't shown up for the plane after the Sabres played Atlanta the other day. In fact, Maurice thought I might know where Ned is. Needless to say, I don't."

"Is that true?"

She bit her lip. "Well, not entirely, I mean, I think I know where he might be but if he isn't there, then I don't know where else he could be."

"Okay, where might he be?"

"We have—or had, when we were together—a cabin in the Laurentians, near Lost River. We often went there off-season and sometimes even snatched an off-day during the season."

"What makes you think he'd be there?"

"I don't. For all I know, he's simply shacked up with some girl in Atlanta."

"Does he do that customarily?"

She shrugged. "I don't know about his love life these days but to my knowledge he's never let it interfere with hockey. I often told him hockey was his real mistress, though that wasn't strictly…" She gulped and waved a wisp of hair out of her eyes. "Anyway, he's never missed a game except for injury."

"Why would he go to this cabin—if that's where he did go?" I looked at her carefully, seeking in her eyes something I suspected she wouldn't reveal with her tongue.

"To think. Or perhaps…" She dawdled over the thought. "Perhaps to hide."

"Hide? What from?"

She arched a brow. "I suspect you might know more about that than I."

"I do," I said. "But I'd prefer to hear what you think."

Our dinner arrived, but she stared down at her plate disinterestedly. I was starved, however, and shoveled broiled swordfish into my mouth as she talked.

"About four days ago Ned called me. He apologized for the scene he'd made up in Montreal. He said, now that we're separated, he has no claims on me and couldn't understand why he got so jealous of you. I suppose it's because…well, it doesn't matter." She poked at a french-fried potato but left it on the end of her fork. "He asked me about you and I told him who you were and what you were doing up there in Montreal. I didn't, of course, tell him…I left out…you know." She took a large gulp of water.

"What exactly did you tell him I was doing in Montreal?"

"I said you'd been asked by Vince Sturdevant to investigate Guy's death."

"What was his reaction?"

"I couldn't see his face over the phone, naturally, but he began asking me a lot of questions. He seemed very excited."

"Excited?"

"Agitated. Upset."

"Did you tell him about the book?"

"Yes, I finally had to. He kept badgering me to find out why we thought Guy might have been murdered."

"What did he say?"

"When I told him about the book? He didn't say anything. In fact…that was the odd thing. After this barrage of questions, suddenly he didn't seem interested in pursuing the book at all. It was as if I didn't really analyze it until later—it was as if he knew about the book." She looked at me bleakly. "Will you please order me a drink? And have them take my food away. I can't stand to look at it." She lit a little cigar. Her eyes, already haunted, looked sunken and ghostly in the flicker of candlelight from the table.

She smoked in jerky puffs, looking distractedly out of the picture window until her drink was brought out. She threw half of it down her throat and took a deep breath. Then she gazed at me, eyes blinking back tears. "Dave, I'm no fool."

"Did I say you were?"

"Ned was involved in that gambling scandal Guy was planning to put in the book, wasn't he?"

"There's no evidence one way or the other—yet."

"But that's what you think, isn't it? That Ned threw a game or something and now that there's an investigation, he's hiding. Hiding or—something's happened to him." She looked desolate. The alcohol and tears were making her eyelids puffy. "Is that possible, Dave? That something has happened to him?"

I gave her my thinking, inadequate though the premises were. It could have been Guy Laclede who threw the playoffs but then why would he reveal this in a book after managing to keep it a secret for years? It could have been Ned but Ned had won three of the four games in which he'd played in the Stanley Cup finals. It could have been Irv Staley, their coach. Or any combination, or all three. Or none.

I told her about Kaleeka and said, "If Ned was involved in the fix, it's very possible something has happened to him. Kaleeka would want to shut him up for good."

"Do you have a cigarette?" Her hands were trembling violently.

"I thought you smoke cigars."

She turned around and bummed a cigarette from a couple sitting behind her, lit it, and inhaled deeply. "Not when I'm in a state like this."

"This cabin of Ned's, does it have a phone?"

"No."

"Did you try getting a message to him? Call the local store up there or something?"

"No. I wasn't sure I should let him know what I suspect.

I wanted to talk to you first."

"What's the best way to get there?"

"Fly to Montreal, then it's a couple of hours by car. I can write out the directions if you're thinking of going there."

"I am." Then I asked Ellen the same questions I'd asked Babette Laclede, questions about Ned's finances mostly. "Did Ned have money troubles before the playoffs? Show signs of being flush after them?"

Her answers were vague and, I thought, even evasive. Ned, she said, didn't have money troubles exactly but often talked of what he'd do if he could somehow make a killing.

"What was that?" I asked.

"Take me away."

"Away? From what?"

"From Chi—Just away. Around the world, or something."

"You were going to say, from Chicago?"

"I hated Chicago."

"Why?"

"I just did."

"You've been holding something back from me," I said, slightly peeved with her. "Don't you think it's time you told me what it is?"

She lowered her eyes and opened her purse. "I'll write down those directions."

"Just answer me one more question, did Ned seem to act like a man who'd made a killing, after the playoffs?"

"He bought me a fur coat," she said, writing instructions in a fine hand on a little pad. "But he said it was paid for out of the ten thousand dollars he got as his loser's share of the playoff money."

"Do you believe that?"

"I don't know what to believe any more, Dave. Please get up to Lost River as soon as possible."

Chapter XI

· · · ·

Vince Sturdevant looked more tired than the last time I'd seen him. Perhaps it was the weariness of having had to oversee the innumerable details of professional hockey for the last eight months but I got the impression the Laclede case had added to his woebegone expression. He chewed grimly on his cigar as he showed me to the deep armchair in front of his television set, to which a bearded young engineer type was attaching a closed-circuit videotape apparatus. "I have a car lined up for you. As soon as the screening is over, you can be on your way. And I've taken the liberty of ordering up lunch."

He called his receptionist and a moment later a cart was wheeled into the office with service for two laid on in silver, crystal, and fine china—onion soup, pheasant, asparagus spears, and glacéed pears. The dishes were placed on low stack-tables in front of us and wine was poured.

The bearded young engineer type, whom Vince introduced as Bob Linsey, made some final adjustments on the videotape machine, plugged a cable into a remote-control console he held in his lap, and said, "Any time you're ready, Mr. Sturdevant."

"Okay, Bob, why don't we start right away?"

"Fine with me," Bob said. "Highlights of the Chicago Black Hawks-New York Rangers Stanley Cup finals, compliments of the National Hockey League."

I pitched into my soup, but soon found myself so absorbed I was able to eat only with difficulty and succeeded in getting more food on my blazer than into my mouth. Two hungrier teams had not been iced in—literally—decades, for the Black Hawks hadn't won a Stanley Cup since the 1960-61 season, and the Rangers, dogged by their jinx of choking in the clutch, since 1939-40. To give an idea of the frenzied anticipation rampant in the two cities, a Chicago scalper had been murdered and robbed for standing-room tickets, and in New York, there'd been a riot outside Madison Square Garden's ticket windows that sent twelve fans and four cops to the hospital.

The teams played a similar brand of hockey, belligerent and aggressive in the pattern established a few seasons earlier by the Philadelphia Flyers in their Cinderella sweep to the Stanley Cup in 1973-74. Both Chicago and New York had had infusions of new blood after the retirement or purging of some of their aging stars and the kids had managed to shake off the losing tradition in which their teams had been mired for so long. New York relied on a sensational young goalie from British Columbia named Bernard Jouet, while Chicago alternated Guy Laclede and Ned Boudreau as it had done through the regular season and earlier rounds of the playoff series. Though neither of the two possessed Jouet's brilliance, they made up for it with steady competence and determination. Chicago also iced the best defensive array in hockey to keep shots on goal to a minimum and those from long distances or difficult angles.

The first game had been played at Chicago Stadium by virtue of the Black Hawks' better overall season record but despite the pandemonium every time a Black Hawk stick touched the puck, the Rangers won the first game 4-1. Guy Laclede had tended goal.

Elbows on knees, I leaned forward to watch the replays of the four Ranger goals. My job was aided by the terrific television coverage of the series, providing slow-motion replays from three different camera angles plus a fourth from behind the net. Bob Linsey, the engineer, obliged me with replays of the replays whenever I wanted a second or third look, and controlled the tape carefully to freeze any moment for my inspection.

Of the four goals scored against Guy Laclede that first game, only one, the fourth, was a candidate for suspicion and that one I ruled out because it happened late in the third period when defeat was already a foregone conclusion. The other three were made, respectively, on a screened slap shot that even the behind-the-net camera didn't pick up until it whizzed past Guy's flailing glove into the net, a deflection which no goalie was fast enough to have reacted to, and a brilliant Ranger power play that caught Guy committing to his right and unable to scramble back left when Andy Miletti, the left wing, faked a slap shot and passed beautifully to his right wing Bud Janacek for the score.

Ned Boudreau minded the net for the second game, which Chicago won 3-2. The first goal against Ned was indisputably real, a treacherous bouncing slap shot that flicked off Ned's stick, hit the top rim of the net, and dropped just inside the line as Ned fell on top of it and scooped it back under his chest. In fact, Ned argued vociferously that the puck had not gone over the line, and seemed purple-faced with rage when he took off his mask to dispute the call.

The second Ranger goal was so interesting I had Bob run it four times. Andy Miletti chased the puck behind Ned's net, came around and centered it just as Bob Fiske on point swooped in from the left. The puck was wobbling when he hit it, and he topped it so that it slid in at half-speed. Ned had braced himself for a hard shot, and when the puck dribbled in he looked like a batter who, expecting a high hard pitch, swings for the seats—only the pitch he gets is a floating change-up. Ned kicked his foot out for a split-save but the puck glided in casually just under his behind. It didn't even have enough force on it to slide to the back of the net. Ned collapsed on the ice as Rangers whizzed past him with sticks upraised, and lay there dejectedly for a full minute.

I turned to Vince Sturdevant. "What'd you think of that one?"

He shook his head and shrugged. "You see goals like that all the time. The goalie commits himself for a bullet and he's stretched to the limit of his body. He can't recover to stop the puck even if it's only creeping at him."

"On the other hand," I said, "it's easy enough to fake."

He rolled his wine around his large crystal goblet. "I don't think any of them are easy to fake. For one thing, unless you've been faking regularly you can't break your reflexes of the habits they've learned since childhood. You automatically move to stop the puck, it's as natural as flinching. You almost don't know how to order your muscles to do anything else. And remember, it's not just letting the puck through, it's looking convincing as hell when you do it. You blow an easy shot and you arouse suspicion. So what we're looking for is a shot that is at once difficult and easy."

We scrutinized games three, four, five, and six until the pattern emerged: Laclede lost every one of his games, Ned won every one of his. Yet both performed so magnificently it was impossible to detect an unnatural note anywhere.

It came down to game seven and now Coach Richard made a critical decision, though it was Guy Laclede's turn in the rotation, Richard, as any coach would, pulled Laclede for his winning goalie, Ned Boudreau.

Bob pulled a toggle and the game unfolded on the big television screen in front of us. Chicago scored first on a short-handed goal with Sonny Batiste stealing the puck for an easy breakaway against Jouet. There was no further score during the first period but in the second the Rangers came out with a rush to hit Boudreau with everything but the George Washington Bridge—sixteen shots on net. Two of them went in and if Boudreau didn't give his all to stop them, I don't know what effort is.

But Chicago came back in the last minute of the period to tie the score at 2-2 with an incredible play by Mindy Jenks, who swept down along the right-hand boards until he was almost parallel with the net, then cut in as sharply as Paul Warfield began running a zig-in pattern. Shielding the puck with his stick while a Ranger defender stabbed at it from behind, he deked Jouet, who lunged. Jenks somehow managed to keep control of the puck and, gliding past Jouet, backhanded it into the net. I hadn't thought it possible for a man to make a ninety-degree turn on skates at that speed, but Jenks did, and for my money, it was the best play of the series.

"Coming up," said Vince, "is the winning goal in the third period with two minutes left. You want to advance the tape to that spot, Bob?"

The television screen flickered with garbled images coveting seventeen minutes of the third period. While we waited for Bob to home in on the critical moment, Vince said, "What do you think now, Dave?"

"I still rule out Guy and for two reasons. For one thing, though he's lost three games, he looked great losing them.

I mean, he broke his heart out there. For a second thing, I still can't figure out why, if he was guilty, he would expose himself in his own book."

"But Ned looks even better, he's won three games."

"Yes, but he may be thinking, 'Why, hell, I don't have to throw any games, Guy is doing my job for me!'"

"So that Ned only has to blow game seven."

"Exactly."

Bob brought the tape down to normal speed and the Stanley Cup-winning play developed.

The Rangers won a face-off in their own zone. Andy Miletti brought the puck up into Black Hawk territory flanked by Bob Fiske at the point with Jerry Binet, the other wing, trailing Fiske. The Black Hawks' two defense-men and their point man, Rogier, fanned out, forcing the attackers to the outside and cutting down their angle. Sud-denly, Miletti stopped on a dime, pirouetted, and flicked the puck to Fiske. Fiske faked a slap shot and when Rogier went for it, Fiske wristed the puck hard at Ned Boudreau. Ned went into a huddle and the shot whizzed in low. He swatted it back with his stick.

Into the slot.

The slot is a zone roughly five by ten feet directly in front of the goalie's crease. Of all the places a goalie can bat a shot back into play, it is the very worst. This was demonstrated an instant later when Jerry Binet, riding Fiske's coattails, collected the carom and, as Fiske peeled off in front of him, blazed it high past Ned Boudreau's ears. A blinding red light behind the net, upraised arms, and the Rangers had their first Stanley Cup in well over three decades.

I looked over my shoulder at Bob Linsey. "Would you mind running Fiske's shot again, and stopping the tape at the moment Boudreau stopped it?"

"Sure."

Bob reversed the tape and we reviewed the play. At the instant Fiske's shot touched Boudreau's stick we froze the tape and gazed at the unmoving image on the screen. "Mr. Sturdevant," I said, "would a goalie of Ned's experience receive a shot from dead center with his stick held parallel to the net that way?"

"Not if he expects to last long in the NHL," Sturdevant replied. "But of course, he may simply have made a misjudgment."

"I doubt it," Bob interjected. He'd refrained from commenting throughout the taping but his restraint only added emphasis to what he said when he finally spoke. "Even schoolkids don't goof like that. It's drilled into them to angle their stick so that the puck caroms away from the slot. Otherwise they're just inviting a score on the rebound. Hell, Ned fed that rebound on a spoon to Billet. I'm surprised the official scorers didn't award Boudreau with an assist."

"Then, gentlemen," I declared, "I would say we may have just witnessed Ned Boudreau throwing the last game of the playoffs."

Bob ran the replays from the other angles. There was still room for doubt, of course, but given all the other factors, I just couldn't excuse Ned's play as a mere blunder.

As we were running it through again the intercom sounded and Sturdevant picked up. "Sally, I thought you were going to hold all...oh, certainly, put her on." He looked at me. "It's Ellen Boudreau. She says it's urgent."

I rose and paced nervously as he talked to her in grave monosyllables. Something was wrong and when Vince asked, "When did they leave?" I knew what it was. "But you're all right?" he then said and when his face reflected relief, I took my first breath since the phone had rung.

"You'd better have a doctor look at it, anyway," he said. "Call me later." He hung up and looked at me miserably. "Kaleeka's men paid Ellen a visit. They roughed her up a little, nothing serious. They made her tell them where Ned's cabin is. They're on the way." He looked at his watch. "Let's see, assuming they caught a plane immediately, they could be here…"

"Uh-uh, I wouldn't figure it that way, Mr. Sturdevant. Kaleeka's been beaten out once by me in an airplane race. This time he may opt to send a crew directly out of Montreal." I jumped to my feet. "I've got to start for Lost River at once."

"Alone?" Sturdevant asked.

"No time to hire recruits even if I could think of where to find some. We don't want to bring in the police."

"No, but…"

"If I can get there ahead of Kaleeka's men and bring Ned out, I won't need help. And if Kaleeka's men get there first, I certainly won't need help."

"You ought to be armed, anyway," Bob Linsey volunteered. "Do you have a gun?"

Before I could answer, Vince threw up his hands. "I don't like it. We're getting into this thing way over our heads."

"Getting? We've been over our heads since the day I walked into Kaleeka's office." I looked at Bob. "No, I have no gun."

"I have a hunting rifle in the trunk of my car. Thirty-thirty with a scope, plus a few boxes of ammunition. Take it. And take me, too."

I looked at Vince Sturdevant, whose head drooped like a dead flower. It was all too overwhelming for a man who desired nothing more than to administer a bureaucracy. He waved his hand in resignation. "Do whatever you want. Another corpse isn't going to make much difference when this thing hits the newspapers."

I studied Bob's face for strengths and weaknesses. It was a gaunt, long face with hollow cheeks obscured by a reddish-brown full beard. He looked like a private-school math teacher but his eyes were steely and he had an outdoor look that contradicted the first impression of a placid, sedentary nature. "You got a family?" I asked him.

"No, I'm just a happy bachelor," he said, smiling. "And a deadly shot."

"Let's go," I said.

CHAPTER XII

· · · ·

We transferred Bob's gear into the Pontiac Firebird Vince Sturdevant had leased for me and nosed into traffic. Bob guided me to the Decade Expressway and we followed it to the Metropolitan Boulevard cloverleaf, where we picked up Route 8. We followed it in a northwesterly direction, through Saint-Hermas and into Lachute, where the highway thinned and we began to climb. Soon we reached Dalesville, where the road branched. A left turn would take us south to Calumet but we wanted to forge farther north, to Lost River. Oiling and polishing his rifle, Bob gave me a rundown of the geological formations that was only half academic, he'd been raised not too far from here, in Saint-Canut, and had a good first-hand familiarity with the countryside.

As we twisted into the high country, I removed my eyes from the road for a moment or two when I got a chance, absorbing the majesty of the rugged escarpment and heavily timbered valleys. It was my kind of country and I realized how long it had been since I'd tramped through wilderness and fished icy mountain streams. "It's called Lost River,"

Bob was saying, "because it runs under a natural limestone bridge, Gate Lake on one side, Fraser Lake on the other. Ned's cabin is probably somewhere in that area."

The town of Lost River itself was a tiny hamlet, scruffy and raw and almost primitive, in contrast to the city of Montreal a mere forty miles away. But we learned what we'd come to learn; a cheerful fat lady in the general store told us Ned had been in for provisions only a few days before. She directed us to his cabin which stood on a ridge overlooking the two lakes.

We snaked up a dirt road that bore through dense, shadowed woods, following a turbulent stream for several hundred yards, then forked away from it, climbing steadily, glimpsing through bright interstices in the pines and firs the gleam of still water. The road now became little more than a dirt track, pitted, stony, and rutted by exposed tree roots as thick as arms. We jounced over it for about a mile, continually ascending until the parameters of the two lakes, like a pair of green eyes, became visible below. Suddenly I glimpsed it, a small split-log cabin covered with tar shingles. I slowed the car to a creep and peered through the trunks of a stand of spindly young Norway pines, whose foliage didn't start until thirty or forty feet up.

At first, I thought the cabin was abandoned. We inched up and I finally caught the red glint of a car. I was fairly certain it was Ned's but we proceeded cautiously anyway until we broke out of the woods. There, on a cleared knoll, stood the cabin, commanding a spectacular view of the valley out of which we'd ascended, a forest so dark green it was almost black.

A weedy double track led up to the house, and I followed it at idling speed, straining my eyes for a sign of life. Then I saw it. It was in the form of another metallic glint. It was blue and it said gun barrel to me. Behind it was Ned.

Leaving the engine running, I tugged the hand brake and got out, instructing Bob to get the hell out of there if there was trouble and call in the police because we'd exhausted all unofficial resources and from here on the matter was better left in the hands of trained authorities.

Keeping my hands well away from my body to show Ned I was unarmed, I walked up the tire-track of flattened grass to within seventy or eighty yards of the cabin. Suddenly a spout of earth kicked up five yards in front of me, succeeded immediately by the echoing report of a rifle. I stopped and held my hands even wider from my hips. "I'm unarmed, Ned. I just came to talk," I shouted.

"Get the fuck out of here, Bolt," he shouted back. "I'll kill you, so help me."

"That won't solve anything, you know that." I advanced another ten paces and stopped. I could see him clearly now, squatting behind a big silver birch that shaded the cabin, fixing me in the telescopic sight of what even from this distance I could tell was a large-bore rifle, one designed for bear or moose or players' agents.

"Not another step, Bolt. This one's aimed at your heart," he yelled.

"Listen to me, Ned," I hollered into a strong gust of wind that pushed the words back into my throat. "Kaleeka's people are on the way up here. They're due any minute. You've got to get out of here right away." There was no answer and I yelled, "I can square things with the League, Ned. They'll keep your secret."

I thought I noticed the gun waver. "Yeah, but they'll never let me play hockey again."

"At least they'll let you live."

"I don't care if I live."

"Your wife does," I answered.

He pondered this a moment, then spat out, "Bullshit."

"She's still in love with you," I yelled. "Believe me."

I stared hypnotically at the barrel of his gun, an ugly black tube focused on my abdomen. It wavered again. I held my breath.

Then it tipped downward. Ned got to his feet and stepped wearily out of the shelter of the tree, rifle cradled the crook of his left arm. He wore a checked flannel shirt and khaki pants, and a wool stocking-cap. His face was grizzled with a salt-and-pepper growth of stubble. His eyes were red and tired, his steps heavy with defeat and indifference.

"You got the script in there?" I asked.

"No."

"Where is it?"

"I destroyed it, of course."

"After you killed Guy?"

"I didn't kill Guy."

"Then how...?"

Before I could finish my sentence the engine of my car howled and twin rooster tails of soil spun out of its rear wheels as it lurched forward and careened up the hill. Bob braked in front of us. "They're coming!"

I cocked my ears and heard the sound of a car above the sighs and squeaks of the trees bending in the wind.

Ned heard it, too. "Quick, park behind the cabin," he barked. The car pounced like a cat and skittered around to the back of the cabin. We followed on the double and entered the cabin, a crude one-room box no bigger than a two-car garage furnished with a couple of bunks, a table and four sturdy chairs, and an antique east-iron pot-bellied Stove. Bob tumbled in a moment later, rifle in hand.

Ned pulled a shotgun down from a rack over the door, broke it to check the load and clapped it shut. He chucked it at me and pointed to a box of shells on a shelf over one of the cots, then ran to the window facing the road. Another window, picture size, provided a panoramic view of the valley and lakes to the west of us. Between the two windows, we commanded two-thirds of a circle but the wall on the north side, the weather side, was our blind spot, and it was close to the woods. Strategically, it was the likeliest site from which an attack against us would be launched. "I don't think all three of us should be in here," Ned said. "I'm going—"

"Uh-uh," I said. "I'd like you to stay in here with me. Bob, you station yourself in the woods to our left."

"Check."

"Don't be afraid to shoot, but if you can avoid killing…"

"Gotcha." He sprinted out the door and Ned and I posted ourselves at the front window, squinting through the Norway pines flanking the road, watching and listening. A minute or two later a twinkle of sunlight danced off a chrome hood ornament about two hundred yards down the road and I detected the hum of an engine over the boom of the wind. Then there was no sound but the creak and rustle of trees.

We waited.

They waited.

They were assessing the lay of the land, trying to figure out the best way to approach without being seen. I was pretty sure they wanted Ned alive, at least until he could tell them if he knew anything about the manuscript and where it was. That meant they'd have to come up rather than try to pick him off with a sharp-shot or lay all-out siege to the cabin.

The cabin stood in the middle of a clearing a hundred yards in diameter except for the ten or fifteen yards behind it separating it from the rise, and a similar distance on the north side separating it from the woods in which Bob was lying in wait. They could not risk exposing themselves with a frontal assault. They would fan into the woods and hit us from there and from the rise, most likely. Still, we had the drop on them.

With Ned at the front window and me at the rear, we waited fifteen minutes. Then another fifteen minutes. An hour. Nothing happened. Nothing moved. No one approached. Ned spoke at last, echoing my conclusion. "They're going to wait until dark."

"Uh-huh."

"One good thing is, they don't know you're here, Bolt. They think I'm alone. That's why I had your friend hide the car behind the cabin."

"But if they come up from behind, over the ridge…"

"They still may not see us in the dark, if those clouds hold." He pointed toward the picture window. A thick mass of gray cloud was rolling in from the west, obscuring the sun and promising to obscure the moon and stars, too. I looked at my watch. It was five, the sun lay about thirty degrees over the western horizon. At this latitude and season, it would probably sink out of view in little more than an hour. Give it another hour or two until it was totally dark. Then they'd come.

Ned lit a cigarette and handed it over to me, lighting another for himself. I prefer cigars but welcomed tobacco in any form at the moment. "What you said outside," he grunted. "I mean, about Ellen. Is that true? She actually told you?"

"There are some things a person doesn't have to say."

He hissed smoke into his lungs and snapped the cigarette out of his mouth. "I don't deserve her."

"You'll get no argument from me there."

He grunted again. "But it was because of her…"

I stared. "She put you up to it?"

"Oh no, no. Hell no. But I wanted to do something for her, something that required a lot of money. I'd treated her badly. I wanted to make it up. I'd met this guy Kaleeka a few times, and he'd told me, if I ever wanted to make some big money... Well, before the playoffs he approached Coach Staley and Guy but they turned him down. Then he came to me. I turned him down, too—until the seventh game."

"How much did he give you?"

"Sixty thousand."

"What did you do with it?"

"It's buried somewhere." He scanned the clearing for signs of movement. The shadow of the cabin thrust out before a fugitive shaft of sunlight gleaming through the cloud bank on the western horizon, almost touching the woods along the road.

"Believe me," he murmured, "it wasn't easy, doing what I did. It went against everything I believed in, everything I'd been trained to do. That was my biggest mistake, thinking I could live with myself afterwards. Even sixty thousand dollars couldn't buy off my conscience. It bugged me so bad, I became impossible to live with. That's why Ellen left me. Funny," he said with a chuckle that was anything but humorous, "I did it for Ellen, and by doing it, I lost her."

"What about the book?" I asked. "How did you find out Guy was writing it?"

He took his time answering. "Someone told me," he finally said.

"Ellen?"

"No, she only told me the other day."

"That leaves Babette Laclede," I said. "Nobody else knew."

He said nothing. The air became palpable with his resistance.

"Why did Babette tip you off?" I pressed. "Why was she protecting you? Was it because you were lovers?"

He lit another cigarette and wreathed himself in smoke and silence, like a dour Navajo in a blanket. But despite his refusal to speak, I was certain I was right. Ellen's ellipses when she referred to Chicago and the bitter, bitchy enmity between her and Babette—they all added up.

"Yes," Ned said at last. "She was in love with me."

"But you were in love with your wife!" I winced. "How do you reconcile…?"

"You don't know Babette," he said. "When she wanted you, she was an animal. No man could resist her."

I could certainly appreciate how a man could be totally devoted to his wife while conducting a torrid affair with Babette Laclede.

"And Guy?" I asked. "He knew about her and you?"

"No. I mean, at the time we didn't think so. But he did. Someone had told him. He knew it all the time but didn't say anything."

"Why not?"

"I don't think he knew how to handle it. He knew it would blow two marriages apart and he wanted to be very certain about what he did before he did it. Also, he was afraid of hurting the team. We were on our way to the playoffs at that time."

"I'm getting to like Guy more and more, the more I hear about him."

"He was a good man," Ned said. His sorrow was genuine. "He didn't deserve any of what he got."

"Including murder."

"He wasn't murdered."

I raised my eyebrows. "You know that for certain?" He peered out of the window again. The sun hung like a big

smoky ball over the fretted Laurentian hills. The clouds
that had been forming across the valley were now roiling
in. The first thump of a squall line rattled the cabin and
made the trees lean drunkenly to the northeast. A few drops
of rain splattered the picture window but the sky seemed
to be holding back.

"Okay," Ned said, "I'll tell you everything. About a
week before he died, Babette finally got a look at the script.
Guy had gotten drunk and fallen asleep soundly over his
typewriter. She read it and put it back on his desk and
tried to pretend nothing had happened. But that business
in there about me—she wouldn't permit him to put that in
the book. She insisted he drop it. They quarreled. It went
on for days. But finally, she prevailed."

"How'd she do that?"

"She could make a man do anything," he said. I couldn't
see his eyes but I knew they must be glowing with the
memory of rapture. "But she didn't understand what it
meant to him, asking him to destroy that passage," Ned
continued. "She was saying she still preferred me over him.
She was rubbing his nose in our love affair."

"Yes, I can see that."

"So that night he took the car and said he was going for
a ride in the hills to clear his head."

Suddenly I understood. "He killed himself!"

Ned swallowed loudly. "Yes."

I silently absorbed it all. Guy Laclede, in giving up to
his wife the exposé of Ned's crime, had also given up the
last vestige of his pride and dignity. Until that incident,
he'd cherished a slim hope that despite everything else
he'd lost, he still had his wife's love, that the affair with
Ned was over emotionally as well as physically. Now he
knew he didn't even have Babette's heart. With nothing

left to live for, the way was clear for him. He took his car up into the Boulder Hills and drove it over an embankment.

"She called me the day his body was discovered," Ned finished, "and told me about the script. I asked her to send it to me. She did, everything but the first three chapters, which Ellen had. I read it and burned it."

CHAPTER XIII

. . . .

We debated whether or not to light the lamps. The glow in the cabin might lull Kaleeka's men into an ambush but it would also destroy our night vision. Ultimately we opted for darkness.

My nervousness rose to its highest pitch in the crepuscular light of dusk. It was easier to see in complete darkness than in this gray haze and I was afraid they might choose this moment to strike. I stared into the murk until my eyeballs throbbed. An occasional bluish flash of heat lightning illuminated the high grass behind the house for a moment but disclosed nothing lurking in it. The hushed air began to fill with the chirps of toads and the poignant whistles of birds bedding down for the night. An owl whooped so artificially I thought it was a signal and perhaps it was. More likely it was my imagination, which had been fed on stories of Indian massacres since early childhood.

Another hour went by, and still they didn't come but it couldn't be long now. Then around nine o'clock, we both started at a cracking noise on the blind side of the house, where Bob was supposed to be. Someone had gotten someone, but it was impossible to discern who was the

cracker and who the crackee. A few minutes of silence,
then the patter of footsteps crunching over frost-frozen
leaves. We braced. Someone was coming up to the cabin.

I was about to shift my attention to the door when I
spied a dark form bellying through the grass along the
ridge behind the house. He was just distinguishable at the
dividing line between earth and sky. I fixed him in the sight
of my shotgun but my hands were trembling violently.

"I think…" whispered Ned, peering into the blackness
in front of the house. He'd sighted another. I didn't dare
turn around for fear of losing sight of the wraith in the
shadows outside, yet someone was lurking close to the cabin and if it were not friend but foe he could burst through
the door and cut us down before we could wheel around.
My shoulder blades itched with the sensation of a slug
ripping through the flesh between them.

All at once, the night exploded with light and sound. A
powerful beam of light flooded the grounds, a klaxon-like
horn and an inhuman shriek shattered the stillness and three
shots close at hand echoed over the valley. Fear hammered at
the wall of my chest and panic constricted my throat. If there
were a Doomsday, this is what it would sound like. Then I
realized what had happened. The man outside the cabin was
Bob. He'd gotten into one of the cars, turned on the headlights,
hit the horn, and fired his gun into the night. If the effect on
me had been terrifying, I could imagine what it must be for
Kaleeka's men. The Chinese had used the technique to deadly
effect in the Korean War, routing American troops simply by
playing on their innate terror of the night. I needed no one to
tell me what to do next and neither did Ned.

The guy who'd been creeping up on the cabin from
the back had dropped flat when the lights went on and
at fifteen yards I could have pulped him. I smashed the

picture window with the stock of my gun, jammed the barrel through the ragged hole, and fired a blast into the grass just in front of him, spraying him with a big gout of dirt, gravel, and buckshot. He got to his feet and dashed around the cabin, fleeing in blind panic toward the car. I spun and dashed out of the door, a rebel yell surging from my throat. Ned tumbled out behind me, screeching and yodeling. A second figure stood up in the grass and broke for the car, too, and a third hurtled out of the woods, firing a pistol blindly behind him as he galloped for the car.

The three converged on the path to the car, and I was just congratulating myself on an easy victory when they stopped abruptly, dropped to a kneeling position, and leveled their guns at us. They were going to take a stand. Now it was we who were at a disadvantage because we were silhouetted in the headlights behind us like ducks at a shooting gallery. "Drop!" I hollered, diving to the earth. I was about fifty yards away when they opened fire. I rolled a couple of times and came up straddled in a prone firing position. At this distance, a shotgun pattern would be too wide to kill but might put some dimples in their flesh. I aimed through the reedy grass at the centermost fireburst and squeezed the second trigger. The gun thundered and somebody yelped like a kicked puppy. A moment later, I heard car doors slamming and an engine starting, then the sweet sound of tires spinning on frost-hardened dirt.

"You guys all right?" I called into the night.

First Ned, then Bob answered, and their black forms eclipsed the beams behind them. "I left one in the woods," Bob said.

"Let's get him and clear out before they decide to come back to collect him."

We trudged into the woods and found him, a short, wide man with a bull neck and thin black hair matted by a big viscous blood clot where Bob had clobbered him with his rifle butt. He was sitting at the base of a tree, head bobbing like a drunken bear's, trying to figure out which muscles activate the legs. We hauled him to his feet, groaning.

Ned and I escorted him to Ned's car and Bob took the other one. Ned directed me to an alternate route around the lakes just in case Kaleeka's men had decided to try to bushwhack us. Then we drove due south to Calumet rather than back on Route 8 and picked up 29 East along the northern edge of the Outaouais. At a town called Cushing, we stopped and marched our captive to a phone booth near a roadhouse and I called Kaleeka again.

In the long silence in which we'd waited for the attack, I'd given a lot of thought to the predicament Ned had put us in by destroying the rest of Guy Laclede's manuscript. I knew that Kaleeka would not believe the script irretrievably lost and might go on a rampage of murder to flush it into the open. He was determined to know what was in the book or else eliminate anyone who'd laid eyes on it. Suddenly an idea had flashed into my head, an idea so good as to be classified as a brainstorm. But in order for it to work, I needed time.

There was a click on the other end of the line after the fourth ring. The gravel voice was now intimately familiar to me. "Hello, Mr. Kaleeka, Dave Bolt here—again. Someone wants to talk to you." I handed the phone to Mr. Five-by-Five.

He looked at me. "What do you want me to say?"

"Say hello, for starters. I'm sure the dialogue will flow naturally from there."

He hesitated, looking like a man standing before a gallows. "Hullo, Mr. Kaleeka. It's Lenny. Yeah. They had an ambush. No, we left Montreal the minute you called, swear to God. I'm sorry. I said I'm sorry, what can I tell you? You said there'd only be Boudreau. Yeah. Yeah." He handed the phone to me. "He wants to talk to you."

I took the phone hack. "I'm beginning to get impatient, Bolt," said Kaleeka.

"I know. It must be kind of frustrating."

"Did you find the script?"

"No, but I know where it is. But I need a little more time."

"Why?"

"Never mind why."

"How much more time you need?"

"Maybe a couple of weeks."

"Why so long?" he growled.

"Because it's...inaccessible."

"Suppose I give you a couple of weeks, Bolt. What then?"

"I'll produce the script and turn it over to you. Until then, you call your boys off. Not that they're very effective, mind you, but they're getting to be a nuisance."

"All right, two weeks. But not one second more. At two weeks plus one second, we come out shooting, and so help me I'm going to erase everyone connected with this thing."

"You're eager to protect your reputation, aren't you?"

"Two weeks, Bolt. Two weeks exactly."

"Two weeks," I said.

CHAPTER XIV

· · · ·

We left Lenny in Cushing to fend for himself, then drove hard along 29, guided by the purple glow of Montreal on the eastern horizon. It was after one in the morning when we rolled into Vincent Sturdevant's long, tree-lined drive.

The Sturdevants occupied a large wooden house in Westmount, the fashionable enclave on the lower of Montreal's twin summits. Set back from the road and obscured by trees and bushes so thick as to be almost tropical, it was a gongoristic structure of gingerbread and filigree. Beneath the low and broiling cloud cover, it looked like the setting for a horror movie. The downstairs lights were ablaze. We'd phoned Sturdevant to tell him we'd survived the siege of Ned's cabin and were returning.

I tapped the huge brass knocker and we waited. Just before the door opened, Ned put a hand on my arm and said, "Remember what you promised."

"I won't forget," I said.

The thick oaken door swung open, flooding the front yard with light. Vince Sturdevant was dressed in slacks, slippers, and a red smoking jacket, and he peered fearfully into the

night before admitting us as if the rhododendrons and aza-
leas might momentarily turn into Mafia button men—which
was by no means a fantastic idea. He whisked us inside.
The thump of the door and the click of locks were the most
comforting sounds I'd heard all night. Even more comforting
was the sight of Sturdevant's wife, a statuesque brunette in
a flowing blue robe who greeted us with a silver tray laden
with steaming coffee in mugs and a pyramid of doughnuts.

We followed her into a green sitting room and her body
momentarily obscured another figure in the room. Then she
stooped to set the tray on a table, revealing Ellen Boudreau
seated near the blazing fireplace. There was a white ban-
dage on her temple and two Band-Aids on her cheekbone.
Her upper lip was puffy around a thin crimson wound
under her nose. Ned stared at his wife with a mixture of
anger and pity, then rushed to her, embracing her before
she could rise to her feet. "Those bastards!"

"You're all right, you're all right," Ellen murmured,
bursting into tears. Bob Linsey and I turned away, feeling a little embarrassed. Vince Sturdevant thumped our
shoulders and made a little speech. Mrs. Sturdevant plied
us with coffee and doughnuts like a Red Cross volunteer at
a disaster site. I glanced at the couple and felt another stab
of jealousy and indignation that Ellen could still care so
deeply for a man who had treated her so shabbily. That was
when it came to me that Ellen was, at base, a masochist,
too dependent on Ned to snap the thralls that bound her to
him, though she knew in her heart that sooner or later he'd
break her heart again.

As Bob and I related the night's events, Ellen sat moon-
ing at Ned like a schoolgirl. It would have been so easy to
shatter that rapture and Ned looked at me anxiously several
times to see if I was going to keep my promise not to tell

Ellen what he had told me. It was not easy to do because at this point I hated Ned with unreasoning ferocity. My biggest test came when Vince Sturdevant asked about the script.

"There is no script," I announced.

"It's been destroyed?"

I was looking at Ned when I answered. "It never existed." Even Ned looked confused for a moment. "Guy never got beyond the three chapters he turned in to Ellen in January," I amplified.

Ellen blinked. "But he told me he was almost finished with it."

"He was lying. He was too busy to work on the script once the hockey season was into full swing. He lied to you because he felt guilty. His hope was to finish it on a crash basis as soon as the season ended."

"Oh, God," Ellen groaned. "Another typical author."

"How do you know this?" Vince asked me.

"Babette Laclede told me."

"And you believe her?"

"Yes."

"And Guy's death?"

"An accident," I said. "Just the way it looked."

Vince scrutinized my face. "You expect me to believe that?"

"Believe it or not, that's what my inquiry turned up."

"And what about…?" He gestured with his thumb at Ned.

"Ned threw the last goal of the last game of the playoff with the Rangers," I said. "It was that that Guy had been planning to expose in his book but he never got that far. The fact that he died in a car accident is pure coincidence. Nobody murdered him."

Sturdevant turned to Ned. "You realize you'll have to quit hockey."

"Yes, sir."

"You're lucky that's as far as it goes."

"Yes, sir."

Sturdevant then looked at me. "Well, I guess that's that."

"But it isn't," I said. "You see, everyone is satisfied except Morty Kaleeka. He doesn't believe there's no script. He's convinced we have it and are going to use it against him."

Sturdevant wiped his brow. "But didn't you tell him…?"

"I told him."

"And?"

"I told you, he doesn't believe me. He's given me two weeks to come up with the script or, to use his phrase, he comes out shooting. I hate it—but the guy's an animal and we can't afford to let this scandal claw its way out of the bag."

"But that's…unreasonable!" Even Sturdevant grimaced at the inadequacy of the word.

"Nobody ever said Morty Kaleeka was rational. But we've got to satisfy him or somebody is going to get hurt."

"How do you propose to produce a script that doesn't exist?" Sturdevant demanded, retreating to the cocktail table for a brandy.

"By 'producing' it," I said. I looked at Ellen. "Ellen, you've been a journalist and now you're in publishing. How long would it take a full-time professional writer to write four or five chapters of a book?"

She searched the ceiling with her eyes. "It depends on how much research he has to do."

"Say he's done his research, or has it all in his head."

She shrugged, "Then I'd say a month or two, maybe less if he were a fast worker with a tight deadline. I've seen some authors turn out five thousand words a day."

"Five thousand words a day. What does that come to in chapters?"

"A chapter could be any length but an average one could be about that long—five thousand words."

"Can you write five thousand words a day?"

She laughed. "I've done it under tight deadlines, but they weren't very good words. On the other hand—ah!" Her eyes flooded with recognition and a wicked, tomboy smile spread over her lips. "I see what you're getting at."

Sturdevant was chomping reflectively on his cigar. "I think I do, too." He pointed the stub at Ellen. "Can you get a sabbatical from your job for a couple of weeks?"

"Yes, of course. But do you think we can bring it off?"

Sturdevant, caught up in the excitement of my scheme, started pacing the room agitatedly. "I think we can. You're a writer, you know your hockey. I'll be glad to put the entire resources of the NHL at your disposal to make the book sound authentic. In fact, I could tell you a couple of anecdotes…" He chuckled uninhibitedly, then drew himself back up to dignity. "Ellen, I not only think you can do it, I think you have to if any of us are going to sleep peacefully from here on in."

CHAPTER XV

· · · ·

Compared to the previous week, the next ten or twelve days were halcyon in their tranquility. In fact, with the cease-fire with Kaleeka in effect, I not only relaxed, I took a short vacation.

No, I did not go to Jones Beach or Hawaii or Las Vegas or Bimini or Ireland or Katmandu. Very simply, I stayed in Montreal and watched television. But not just any television, I watched the NBA and NHL playoff games. As I said before, everyone has his sickness, and the play-offs are mine. Watching NBA and ABA playoffs, Stanley Cup playoffs, the World Series, the World Cup, the Super Bowl—that's how I get off. Sue me.

I stayed in Montreal in order to be close to Ellen, who was ensconced in a guest room in Vince Sturdevant's home, writing "Guy Laclede's" book on an old Remington portable identical to the one Guy Laclede had used.

The book was good, not just good as a book but good in its imitation of Guy's style and even his typographical technique. A look at any page bespoke a man completely ill at ease with a machine which, unlike a hockey stick, had moving parts. And the stories!

"Where did you get these?" I asked her one afternoon.

"Some I knew," she replied, "some Mr. Sturdevant gave me—and some I made up."

"This one about Larry Jeannette phoning in a bomb scare to Trudeau's office—is that true?"

"I'm afraid it is. Larry is fanatical about French-Canadian autonomy. He won't, you know, speak English to anybody, not even his teammates."

"Jesus. And this, this practical joke Billy Padrewski played on Bobby Orr?"

"I made that up," Ellen laughed, "but if you knew Billy, you'd know he was capable of doing it and probably has. He once snuck into the San Francisco Seals locker room and padlocked every locker."

I shook my head. "It's a shame this book will never see the light of day. It's being written to be destroyed."

"I only want to reach one reader," Ellen said. "If he swallows it, it's worth more to me than a year on the bestseller list."

She pushed away from her desk and stretched, her breasts tracing graceful arcs from her neck to her abdomen. Then she went limp like a ragdoll and yawned.

"You've really been knocking yourself out," I said, putting my hands on her shoulders and kneading the muscles.

"Mmm, thanks, that's delicious." She flexed her shoulders and I could feel the tight ligaments relaxing under my palms.

"I hope you believe he's worth it," I said. I'd wanted to say it for a long time.

"Well, it's not just Ned's skin I'm saving."

"That's ducking the question." I massaged the nape of her neck and she twisted her head from side to side, murmuring sensually. My backrubs are bonafide turn-ons for some women.

"Ned's my husband," she finally said.

"That's still ducking the question. Are you afraid to tell me you still love him?"

She turned in her chair and faced me. "I suppose I am, a little."

"Because you care for me?"

She looked away, blinking rapidly. "Yes, but I'm afraid you'll misinterpret that."

"You mean, you care for me because of what I've done for Ned."

"Yes, but even more because of what you've done for me."

"I'm not sure I—"

"I mean," she said, "lying to spare my feelings."

I gulped. "Lying?"

"About what really happened to the script."

I felt my face reddening.

"Babette found it, didn't she?" Ellen pursued.

"Yes."

"And she destroyed it?"

"Not exactly. She made Guy give it to her."

"She gave it to Ned, then."

"Yes."

"And he destroyed it."

"Yes."

"How did Guy really die?"

"He killed himself. He was despondent about giving up the script."

"Despondent!" Ellen exclaimed, putting her hand to her mouth. "But why…?" The question answered itself even as she asked it. "Ah, because of what it meant to him to give her the script."

"Yes."

"She took everything from him."

"Yes."

She buried her face in her hands. "Oh, poor Guy," she sobbed.

"He died for our sins," I said closing the door quietly behind me.

The plane touched down at 1:15 p.m., the impact jolting me out of a deep, dreamless nap. I stared stupidly at the other passengers sliding prematurely into the aisle before the plane reached the terminal. Another eight or ten minutes and the jets whined to a halt.

I slid out of my seat and reached for the overhead rack to get my raincoat. My right arm jerked and I remembered the briefcase was handcuffed to my wrist. I inched down the aisle behind a fat mother with two pudgy sons, then through the gantlet of goodbye-saying stewardesses and onto the covered ramp to the terminal gate. Outside, rain thundered onto the tarmac in great smoking sheets.

There was a thick crowd around the gate but had it been as jammed as the Broadway Local at rush hour, I'd have been able to pick my welcoming committee out as quickly and surely as I did now. Not that they dressed like Damon Runyon plug-uglies with dark shirts and white ties and wide-lapeled jackets and broad-brimmed hats, nor did they flip half-dollars into the air or pick their teeth with a stiletto. They dressed more like civil service workers on their day off, in dark double-knit slacks, check shirts, shiny black shoes, and raincoats over their arms. It was in the darting, aquiline scrutiny of those eyes that I knew these were my escorts; they roved over every face and typed each instantly as friend, foe, or neutral. One of them spotted me and elbowed the other. They stepped forward.

"Bolt?" This was the shorter of the two.

"That's me."

"May we help you with your luggage?" He put his hand on my briefcase and tugged firmly. I released it and my arm came with it.

"Help yourself," I said. They looked at each other uncertainly and I said, "I told Mr. Kaleeka I'd hand it over to him in person."

"All right, come with us. You got any other luggage?"

"I wasn't planning to spend more than a few hours."

They exchanged amused glances and the short one said, "That ain't up to you, pal."

Flanking me like a guard of MP's, they led me through the terminal toward the garage. I looked wistfully in the direction of the lockers, realizing I had a gun still stashed in one of them. There was no way I could get it, and even if I could, it would be frisked off me long before I might have use for it. Stoically, I let them hustle me through the automatic double doors to the garage. The tall one trotted off to get the car. "How do the Cardinals look this year?" I said to the other.

He seemed surprised by my apparent indifference and muttered something about Bob Gibson's arm. It was quite humid in the garage and we both perspired profusely. A powder-blue Cutlass swung around and my man ushered me into the back seat. We passed through the garage's toll gate, then immediately pulled onto a little grass island, where the short one frisked me.

He reached into my pocket and pulled out a ring of keys. "Which one unlocks those irons?"

"None of them," I said. "The one you want is in my rectum. Would you like…?"

"Never mind," he said, commanding his friend to drive on.

We turned right at the airport exit and got on a highway to St. Louis but got off almost immediately as the scaffolding of a half-built apartment complex thrust its jagged profile into the rainy sky on the right. This was the construction site I'd passed a month ago on my first visit. The building had gone up fast.

We turned into the site behind a cement truck and jounced over a plank road through a series of security gates until we arrived at a four-car train of house-sized trailers constituting the on-site office of Kaleeka Construction Company. We parked in front of the third of these and slopped through an inch of mud.

Kaleeka, in shirtsleeves and orange hard-hat, was poring over a blueprint unrolled over a thick piece of plywood trestled across a pair of wooden horses. He glanced up at me and said, "You're twelve hours late. That could have been costly."

"I was counting on your reputation as a man of compassion," I said.

He looked at the manacles shackling the briefcase to my wrist and at the combination lock clinching the briefcase shut. Then he looked at me and said, "Let me teach you a lesson in compassion. Billy, you got your knife?"

The taller of my two companions reached into his pocket and pulled out a switchblade that was only a little shorter than a javelin. He tossed it to Kaleeka, who flicked it open and stepped close to me.

"Don't you think chopping my arm off at the wrist is excessive?" I said.

"Excessive?" He gripped my wrist in stubby, powerful fingers and honed the knife against the flesh of my forearm. A fine fuzz of blond hair piled up along the edge of the blade. "I don't think it's adequate, considering the inconvenience you've caused me."

I tried to look cool but my heart was thundering like Haitian tom-toms on sacrifice night, and the skin on my handcuffed wrist was tingling with anticipation of the quick slash which would part flesh from bone as easily as a butcher trimming beef from a shank. I looked into Kaleeka's eyes and found a chilling absence of emotion.

He held the blade up to the ceiling light fixture, contemplated it with admiration, then flashed it at my wrist in a silver arc.

It razored through the leather of my briefcase as if it were made of bed linen.

I took a deep breath and let it out slowly with a silent prayer of thanksgiving. "I'm glad you didn't go in for obstetrics," I said.

"This is my baby," he replied, reaching into the wounded bag and pulling out the manuscript. He waved his aides out of the trailer. "Hang around, boys. I may need you to shovel Mr. Bolt's remains into the truck going out to the landfill."

He laid the script on the trestle table over the blueprint and set the open knife beside it. I lowered myself onto a wooden stool and watched him thumb page after page looking for the passage that interested him.

"It's towards the end, around page one-sixty," I said.

He turned over a thick chunk of pages, shuffled through several more, then leaned over the script tensely. His eyes darted over the page, then slowed to a crawl. He flipped the page and examined the one beneath it. Slowly his eyes traveled the length of the sheet, and an expression of dismay came over his face, broadening with each new page he read. Finally, he looked up at me. "This is it?"

"Yes."

"This is all of it?"

"Uh-huh."

He removed his hard-hat and scratched his bald head. "This is cockydoody."

I scratched my own scalp. "Is that good or bad?"

"I've been eating my heart out for this?"

"You sound disappointed."

"Disappointed," he said distractedly, rereading the passage. "Yeah, I'm disappointed, only because I was looking forward to cutting your heart out." He let out an odd cackle, reached for the phone on a file cabinet behind him, and dialed a number. "When I think of what I went through..." he muttered, half to me and half to himself. "Mr. Napolitani, please," he said aloud. Then, to me as he waited, "This is what you call an exposé? This book won't sell five copies if the rest of it is as...Yeah, I'll wait." He thumbed through another section. "Did Larry Jeannette really phone in a bomb scare to Trudeau?"

"That's what it says there."

"Fuckin' lunatics, athletes. They're flakier than broads if you ask me. But at least that's interesting, that story about Jeannette. But this...!" He slapped the section referring to the scandal.

"That's cockydoody," I said. I made a note to ask Trish exactly what that meant.

I heard a click on the phone. "Hello, Mr. Napolitani. It's me. Yeah, I got it and do you want to hear? It's bullshit. Pure, unadulterated bullshit. Nah, the guy copped out. You ready? Listen."

He put the phone down and separated the pertinent section from the rest of the manuscript. "All right, you listening? It says here, 'Earlier in the book I described a number of instances of petty gambling among hockey players. To be fair to my colleagues, ninety-nine percent are completely honest and would never dream of making so much as a nickel bet with each other on the outcome of a game, let alone putting money down with professional gamblers. And though I don't know many players in other professional sports, I'm pretty certain the percentage runs about the same way.

"'Not that many players aren't tempted,'" the script continued. "'But to their thinking the penalties for getting caught—suspension, expulsion, maybe even a prison sentence—invariably outweigh the rewards, and they keep their noses clean. However, there's always that one or two percent who can't resist "getting down" if they think they can get away with it.' I'm sorry, Mr. Napolitani, I'm getting to it now," Kaleeka apologized. "Let's see…" He skipped a page describing some minor gambling infractions, then smiled.

"'But none of these,'" he resumed reading aloud, "'comes close to what happened in the finals of the Stanley Cup playoffs a few years ago. The teams happened to be ancient rivals, and their hunger for the trophy had been whetted by some bitter feuds between a number of the antagonists. It was shaping up to be the hardest-hitting playoff in years. But unknown to any but a handful of men, the outcome had already been decided. For one of the goalies had been paid a lot of money to lose the series.'"

I could hear the phone barking as Napolitani asked Kaleeka a question. "No, Mr. Napolitani, that's the whole point. He doesn't say who the teams are, he doesn't say who the goalies were, he doesn't say who set the deal up, he doesn't say when it took place—it's pure bullshit! Listen."

He picked up the script again and read into the phone. "'The biggest obstacle to the success of this scheme was the goalie's teammates, who redeemed each loss with a magnificent comeback. Thus the series went the full distance, to the seventh game. It was late in the third period, and the score was tied. The visitors came tearing down the ice…blah blah blah.'" Kaleeka tossed a couple of pages over his shoulder. "'He performed the feat so believably, only a few people suspected he hadn't given his last ounce of effort to snatch victory from the jaws of defeat.' Now, Mr. Napolitani, get what he says next: 'Because this assertion is impossible to document, I've been advised by my attorneys to withhold the details of this episode to avoid a libel suit, even though I know it to be true. But the principals know who I'm talking about, and so do the front office executives of the goalie's team, and I wouldn't be surprised if the top brass of the NHL know it, too. But because the image of hockey is more precious to them than the old-fashioned virtues of truth and integrity, I'm certain they'll deny all this as forcefully as they've denied and suppressed so many other injurious stories. But the puck is in their zone. If they have the guts they were born with, they'll launch a proper investigation and come down with both feet on those who would sell out this most exciting of sports for a handful of silver.' That's it. I swear to God, Mr. Napolitani, that's it. Right! Exactly what I said." This was followed by a series of grunted monosyllables. Then, "He's here right now. What do you want me to tell him? Uh-huh. Uh-huh. Then can I take him out and shoot him?" He smiled at the reply and hung up.

He stepped out from behind the table, script in hand, and stuffed it back into the rent in my briefcase. "Here, it's not worth the price of a match to set it on fire. But we still don't want it published. Even something as innocuous as this could arouse the public and make them demand an investigation. So I'll make you a proposition, you drop the book, I'll take my marbles out of hockey."

"For how long?"

"Till I think it's safe to get back in, though I really wonder why I bother with this cockamamie sport. I can make more dough on one Sunday during football season than I can make in six months of hockey."

I put out my hand to shake. The briefcase swung through the air, still attached to my wrist, and almost hit Kaleeka in the nuts.

"Why don't you get out of here, Bolt, before you do some real damage?"

"Sure. But what did Napolitani say about shooting me?"

"He said I shouldn't shoot you, I should offer you a job."

"Thanks. You've made me feel very wanted these last few weeks."

CHAPTER XVI

· · · ·

I walked down the corridor of the Lincoln Building and paused outside my suite to listen at the door. A swell of anxiety rolled through my chest as I contemplated what dreadful carnage might lie on the other side of the door. I pictured another mountainous pile of unfiled folders, scribbled messages, unpaid bills, and new, gruesome, unassayable stains on the carpet.

But all I heard was the comforting clack of two typewriters. I opened the door a crack and peered in.

Trish sat primly at the typing table of the reception desk. On the desk itself lay a neat stack of letters for my signature and a little pile of phone memos squared off like a deck of cards. Except for a vase of yellow tulips, the desktop was uncluttered, and the glass shone. Her In box had one or two items in it, her Out box three or four more. I shouldered the door open a little wider. The visitor's couch was clean and dusted. The rug was in pristine condition. Beyond, in the alcove where he'd been set up with his own desk and phone, Dennis was typing conscientiously. The office had a clean, freshly dusted sheen and a faint aroma of lemon-scented furniture wax. I opened the door and entered.

"Dave! Hi!" Trish rose and extended her slim white arm.

I looked around. "How're things going?"

"Fine, fine. All systems go. Hey, Dennis!"

Dennis came in with a glad hand. "What do you say, Dave?"

"I say...great! I was expecting...well...something else." The two smiled sheepishly. I went into my office. It was tidy and dustless, almost antiseptic. Oddly, I felt a nameless uneasiness growing in the pit of my stomach. The whole thing was too good to be true. The transformation of the office from dungheap to Model Working Environment, the quiet efficiency and cordiality of my two employees, who only a short while ago would cheerfully have broken each other's heads—it was kind of ominous and unnerving.

I asked Trish to step in. She was dressed quietly in cotton slacks and a blousy, unrevealing shirt. "Trish, what's going on?"

She knitted her eyebrows. "What do you mean?"

"I mean, it's like a goddam tomb around here. And you're wearing a bra."

"Gee, Dave, make up your mind. Either you're unhappy because the place is a mess or you're unhappy because it's not."

"What's been happening with your clients?"

"You mean my gals? Well, except for one, they're all signed up, and I've already lined up some appearances for them. I'm negotiating a big multi-year contract for—"

"Except for one, you say?"

She pressed her fingertips together. "Um, yes."

"Who's that?"

She laughed, nervously I thought. "Well, uh, you'll know in about fifteen minutes."

"Huh?"

"She's coming up here. I set up an appointment for you." She fumbled with her fingers.

"Why the mystery?"

"No mystery, just—uh, a little problem, that's all."

"What kind of problem?" I heard the edge in my own voice.

"Hm?"

"You heard what I said. What kind of problem?"

Dennis drifted in front of the door. "Hey, Dennis," Trish called to him, "you want to come in here a sec?"

Dennis lumbered in, looking like he'd swallowed a piece of raw fish.

"Dennis," Trish said, "Dave here has been asking about…uh…our friend."

He grinned a phony, chimpanzee-like grin. "Oh, you mean, uh—"

My temper began to boil. "Hey, look, you. guys, would you mind telling me just what the hell is going on?"

Dennis flapped his arms. "Nothing to get excited about, Dave. See, there's this…uh, you may have heard, or maybe read, about…uh…"

Before he could finish his sentence though at the rate he was going, there was no guarantee he ever would finish it—the door opened and a black man and woman stepped into the anteroom. The man was slightly built and conservatively dressed in an expensive gray three-piece suit and wide silk tie. He wore horn-rimmed glasses and had a low hedgerow of kinky hair around a receding hairline. He carried a highly polished black attaché case. The whole image shouted Lawyer.

The woman, dressed in a quiet, dignified dark suit, plain blouse, and costume circle pin, stood almost a full head higher than her attorney, which put her at about six-three—my own height. She was bigboned but not overweight and reminded me of Althea Gibson, the amateur tennis champ of the late Fifties who ran over her opponents like a panzer division.

I studied her face, a tightly controlled, slightly belligerent one with dark, distrustful almond eyes, and tried to identify her. I knew I'd seen her recently, prominently displayed in a magazine or newspaper, but sometimes when a player is out of uniform it's impossible to identify him—or her—though you've seen him—or her—a thousand times.

Trish and Dennis regarded me with a look of dread, and I still didn't understand why until Trish sang, "Ah, there's Deneen now!"

There's got to be a word for a combination of gape, gawk, gulp, and gag. Whatever that word is, I did it. "Deneen Prior!" I whipped around and glowered at Trish. "How could you do this to me?" My whisper carried just short of my guests' ears.

I looked out at them, smiled and waved cordially, and said, "I'll be right with you." Then I looked at Dennis. "You're in on this, too, aren't you? I knew I smelled a conspiracy the minute I walked into the office."

He looked down at his feet. "Well, Dave, she is a sister. And one helluva athlete."

"You mean one helluva headache."

"I don't call a .366 batting average, seventy-six stolen bases, and only three errors last season a headache."

"But that was for a minor-league team. Not the Detroit Tigers."

"She could hold her own with any major-league ballplayer playing today," Dennis snapped back.

"Hold her own what?"

"That's not funny," Trish said between clenched teeth. "If you lose this client with chauvinistic remarks like that—"

"I'd love nothing more than to lose this client."

"Well, you're not going to if I have anything to say about it."

"The Supreme Court will have something to say about it," I replied.

"She's gonna win her suit and they'll force the Tigers to play her."

"I heard on the grapevine," Dennis said, "that the Commissioner is putting pressure on the Tigers to give her a try. He thinks baseball could lose the suit. Hell, they've lost all the others." He looked out at the reception area, where Deneen and her lawyer were pacing restlessly. "At least hear her out, Dave. She could do for women in baseball what Jackie Robinson did for blacks."

"Yeah, well, I'd like to do for her what Jack the Ripper did for the feminist movement. Show her in."

Dennis and Trish winked conspiratorially.

I composed my facial muscles into something resembling a warm smile and extended my hand to the woman most likely to be the first female to play major-league baseball.

"It's a great honor, Mizz Prior," I beamed, offering her a chair.

A Look At: Strike Zone
(The Pro Book Three)

• • • •

Sports agent Dave Bolt is there to sweep the drug problems, the corruption, and the sex scandals of professional athletes under the rug.

When baseball's biggest rising star, Willie Hesketh, declares he is going to cross the picket line to play the game he loves, someone doesn't agree.

Before Willie even has a chance to arrive at the battle, four thugs with bats ambush him. Now Willie is laid up in the hospital with a slim chance of walking again. All he knows is that he believes he put out the eye of one of the goons and he begs Bolt to get revenge.

It is a twisty road through the maze of managers, union leaders and players, but sports agent Dave Bolt refuses to back down.

AVAILABLE OCTOBER 2020

About the Author

••••

Though Richard Curtis is best known as a leading New York literary agent, he is also author of dozens of works of fiction and nonfiction published by leading publishers, as well as numerous works of humor and award-winning satire. His plays have been performed in numerous venues and festivals in New York. He is currently writing, producing and directing The Creepery, a series of horror podcasts scheduled for launch late in 2020.

Curtis's interest in emerging media and technology led to his founding of the first commercial e-book publishing company in the English language seven years before the introduction of the Kindle and the Digital Revolution.

Curtis was the first president of the Independent Literary Agents Association and was President of the Association of Authors' Representatives in 1996 and 1997.

Early in his freelance career he conceived The Pro, featuring a sports agent sleuth and action hero (modeled after Dallas Cowboys quarterback Don Meredith). Unlike his book's hero, Curtis is not very good with his fists.